The White Giraffe Series

The White Giraffe
Dolphin Song
The Last Leopard
The Elephant's Tale

The Laura Marlin Mysteries

Dead Man's Cove
Kidnap in the Caribbean
Kentucky Thriller
Rendezvous in Russia

The One Dollar Horse Trilogy

The One Dollar Horse
Race the Wind
Fire Storm

The Glory

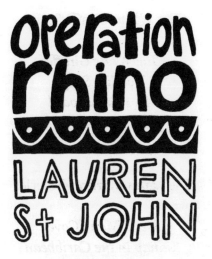

operation rhino

LAUREN St JOHN

Illustrated by David Dean

Orion
Children's Books

First published in Great Britain in 2015
by Orion Children's Books
An imprint of Hachette Children's Group
Part of Hodder & Stoughton
Carmelite House
50 Victoria Embankment
London EC4Y 0DZ
An Hachette UK Company

A CIP catalogue record for this book is available from
the British Library.

ISBN 978 1 4440 1272 9

2 4 6 8 10 9 7 5 3 1

Typeset by Input Data Services Ltd, Bridgwater, Somerset

Printed in Great Britain by Clays Ltd, St Ives plc

MIX
Paper from
responsible sources
FSC
www.fsc.org
FSC® C104740

www.laurenstjohn.com
www.orionchildrensbooks.com

Dedicated to the memory of Carrie the Brave (17/10/99 – 15/09/12), who identified deeply with Martine and was passionate about creating a better world for rhinos and other animals.

'Race you to the bottom of the hill,' said Ben, reining in Shiloh, his new pony. 'Last one there washes the dishes after breakfast.'

Martine brought her white giraffe to a halt by tugging on his silvery mane. She sometimes wondered what would happen if Jemmy ever took it into his head to ignore her; to simply carry on galloping deeper and deeper into the wilds of Africa until she was never heard of again.

After all, it wasn't as if he wore a bridle or saddle, or had spent even a single day being trained, like a horse, to respond to various commands. Although still young he was already nearly five metres high, which meant that

Martine, perched on his withers, would crash a bone-breaking three metres if anything went wrong. And yet riding the white giraffe was the thing she adored most and the place she felt safest. From the moment she'd first encountered him almost a year earlier, when he'd come plunging out of the darkness to save her from a striking cobra, he'd treated her as if she was as fragile as a newly hatched bird. As far as Martine was concerned, the bond between them and the love they had for each other was the best insurance policy any rider could wish for.

'So how about it?' Ben gazed up at her with an innocent expression. 'I mean, Jemmy's legs are at least three times as long as my pony's so the odds are in your favour, but, hey, I'm willing to take the chance.'

Martine shook her head at her best friend's cheek. 'Do you really think I blew in with yesterday's rain shower? I may not be an expert on horses, but even I know that you and Shiloh will fly down the escarpment and reach the road before Jemmy and I have taken two steps. How about racing all the way to the big yellowwood tree near the waterhole? That would be more fair. You might be quicker on the downhill section but at least I'll have a chance to catch you on the plain.'

He laughed. 'Okay, but on one condition. If you lose, you have to do the dishes for the next two weeks.' Gathering his reins, he squeezed the pony's sides. 'Ready? Steady? See you at the waterhole.'

And with that he was off, cantering Shiloh the short distance to the start of the steep trail and disappearing over the edge at speed.

'Ben, wait,' cried Martine. 'Remember to take the track through the trees when you get near the house. If my grandmother catches us tearing around the game reserve, she'll murder us.'

But her words were lost on the African breeze. Ben was already being whisked down the steep trail by his pretty pony, a surprise Christmas present from his parents the previous week. His Indian mum had made a garland of flowers and silk ribbons to put around Shiloh's neck, and his dad, a tall, handsome Zulu who captained a ship, had stunned his son by leading the mare right to the kitchen at Sawubona. She was a Basotho, a hardy mountain breed native to the Kingdom of Lesotho. At the time, Ben had been helping Martine and her grandmother, Gwyn Thomas, prepare a big lunch. He'd looked up from a pan of roast potatoes to see the pony leaning over the door. Even now he kept stroking Shiloh's bay coat in wonder, unable to believe that she was his.

Martine always got a double set of presents because her birthday was on New Year's Eve. She'd loved all of them. Her grandmother had given her a pair of tan leather boots for bush-walking, two pony books and jodhpurs with a special pad sewn into the rear to make riding Jemmy more comfortable. And yesterday, at her birthday brunch, Ben and his parents had given her some much-needed new jeans.

But for Martine, nothing could top the thrill of seeing Ben's face when Shiloh had come prancing up the driveway on Christmas morning. Despite the fact that he'd only learned to ride a few months earlier, he was a born horseman. Horses responded to him the way that wild animals responded to Martine, as if they spoke the same language.

Shiloh would be living in the paddock behind her house, which meant that Ben, who was an apprentice tracker to Tendai, Sawubona's game warden, would be spending even more time at the reserve than he already did. Martine couldn't wait. He'd be able to keep her company when she rode Jemmy, her white giraffe. Instead of them both struggling to stay aboard Jemmy (Ben always joked that it gave him vertigo), they'd be free to explore Sawubona whenever they liked.

'That's what *you* think,' her grandmother had retorted when Martine made the mistake of saying it out loud. 'Just because you're starting high school in a couple of weeks' time, doesn't mean you're suddenly grown-up and allowed to run wild around the reserve. There'll be no night rides, except on very special occasions, and no rides anywhere unless you clear it with Tendai and me first. No, don't look at me like that. As you and Ben understand better than anyone, the game reserve can be a deadly dangerous place.'

It's also the most beautiful place on earth, Martine thought now as she gazed out over the rose-tinted contours of Sawubona. At dawn, a lacy veil of mist made a mystery of the distant waterhole and every forest and valley on the reserve. As the hot pink sun heaved itself above the horizon, the buffalo, zebra and kudu drifted slowly onto the plains, followed by the elephants, trunks still dripping after an early morning bath.

4

In the still-dark caves of the Secret Valley, the leopards retreated to doze away the day until they could once more prowl the night. Out in the open a pride of lions with fat full bellies flopped down on a rise and waited for the sun to warm their tawny flanks. Provided she didn't fall off, Martine was perfectly safe on Jemmy because she was high up, but Ben on a horse was a different story altogether. They kept well away from what Gwyn Thomas called the 'carnivore' section of the reserve in case they inadvertently became breakfast.

Almost the best part about the dawn parade of wildlife was the soundtrack. Over thirty different species of birds serenaded the new day. Tendai had taught Martine to identify some of them. Easiest to recognize was the Heuglin's robin, which sounded the first exquisite notes of the morning at around four forty-five, but her favourites were the shy cooing doves and the thrush with his high, pure song. The flycatchers, warblers, bulbuls and white-eyes were the back-up singers in a choir where the tenor birds – the turacos and trogons, the melodic shrikes and the whistling cuckoos – were the stars.

Listening to them, Martine fancied that they were providing the background music for her race against Ben, especially since Jemmy started to paw the ground beneath her, eager to go after Shiloh. The unlikely pair had almost instantly become friends.

'Jemmy, I'm counting on you to give this all you've got,' Martine told the giraffe. 'I hate doing the dishes. No way do I want to be stuck washing them for the next two weeks.'

The giraffe responded with such enthusiasm that Martine had to fling her arms around his neck to keep from falling off. When he reached the rocky descent he slowed and became awkward, his long gangly legs reaching tentatively for the next foothold. Martine leaned back to take her weight off his shoulders, clinging on with her legs. As she'd predicted, Ben had already reached the plain below. Shiloh was picking up speed, a pale plume of dust rising from her flying hooves.

Martine was impatient to go after them, but she dared not hurry Jemmy. One missed step could be disastrous. By the time they reached level ground Ben and the pony were a distant blur.

Jemmy was as keen to catch them as Martine was. She barely had to touch his sides and he was off, moving from zero to 50 kilometres per hour so fast that it took Martine's breath away. She crouched forward like a jockey, trying not to think about the hard earth flashing by so far below.

Giraffes only have two strides – walking or galloping – but to Martine, at least, Jemmy's gallop was racehorse-fast. His huge stride gobbled up the distance between her and Ben. Faster and faster they went. The wind whistled in her ears. It was like riding Pegasus. A herd of buffalo flashed by. Zebras scattered. Springbok performed epic, slow-motion leaps.

A feeling of freedom so intense that it made Martine giddy flooded through her. Not so long ago she'd been unable to imagine ever being happy again. On New Year's Eve, a year and one day ago – a day that also, cruelly, happened to be her birthday – her mum and dad had died in a fire at their home in England. In the months that followed, the pain in Martine's heart had been so excruciating that often she'd wished that she had died too. Moving to South Africa's Eastern Cape to live with a grandmother she'd never heard of hadn't helped either.

At first, Martine had been so lonely that night after night she'd cried herself to sleep. All she'd had to hold on to was her memories.

Finding Jemmy and learning how to ride him had saved her life. In a way, they'd saved each other, because later Martine had rescued the white giraffe from poachers.

But it wasn't only Jemmy and her friendship with Ben that had helped heal her. It was time, sunshine and a series of tiny miracles, such as the music of Take Flight, her favourite band. Lead singer Jayden Lucas had lost his own father when he was a small boy and whenever she listened to him sing 'Song for Dad' she felt he understood.

Equally important was her relationship with her mum's mum. Cold and strict at first, mainly because she too was grieving, Gwyn Thomas had ultimately proved herself to be the most loving grandmother anyone could wish for.

Another life-saver was Grace, Tendai's aunt, a traditional healer known as a *sangoma*. Within hours of her arrival in Africa, Grace had informed Martine that she was the possessor of a secret gift. That gift had already shaped Martine's destiny and she knew it would continue to do so far into the future. It was a beautiful gift but it came at a high price. Over the past year, it had brought Martine and Ben, who'd accompanied her on every adventure, joy and terror in equal measure.

Racing across Sawubona's glorious plains, Martine was as happy as she'd ever been. There'd always be a hole in her heart in the place where her parents had been, but every day the pain was getting less. Every day she was getting stronger.

'Come on, Jemmy,' she urged, clinging tightly to his mane, 'you can go faster than that.'

The giraffe thundered across the plain, his shimmering white coat and cinnamon-tinged patches lighting up the landscape. They were gaining on Ben and Shiloh. Soon they were so close they could hear the pony's rapid-fire hoof beats. The waterhole came into view. Ahead, the trail forked.

Too late, Martine remembered to remind Ben to go left through the trees. A high fence just beyond the waterhole was all that separated them from her grandmother's immaculate front garden.

'Ben, no . . . !'

It was too late. He'd gone right.

Martine was faced with a split-second choice. Abandon the race and wash the dishes for weeks, or risk incurring her grandmother's wrath. She decided to chance it.

With a squeeze of her left leg, she sent the white giraffe plunging in pursuit of the Basotho pony. In another couple of strides, he'd overtaken Shiloh. Martine grinned over her shoulder at Ben. When she faced forward again, the yellowwood tree was so close she could see the grooves on its bark. Victory was within her grasp.

She glanced in the direction of the house and almost had a heart attack. Was that Tendai standing in the shadows of a mango tree? What if he told her grandmother? She'd be banned from riding Jemmy for the next ten years. But when she looked again there was nobody there.

Shiloh, meanwhile, was in no mood to give up the fight. Though lathered with sweat, she was enjoying every second. Ears flat against her head, she streaked forward until her flaring red nostrils were level with Jemmy's silver ones. The pony and giraffe matched each other stride for stride. The trunk of the yellowwood tree flashed by.

'Photo finish,' Ben said with a grin as his pony puffed to a stop. He leaned down to loosen the girth. 'Too close to call. Although I'm pretty sure that me and Shiloh won by a whisker.'

'You wish,' retorted Martine. 'Jemmy won by at least a nose.'

Laughing and teasing one other, they made their way past the waterhole in the direction of the garden gate. Usually a boy of few words, Ben was bubbling over.

'Did you see Shiloh go? Wasn't she amazing? I mean, I know she's only been mine for a few days but I don't believe that there's a better pony in the whole of South Africa. She's so willing and responsive and, of course, lightning fast . . .'

Martine smiled at Ben's enthusiasm. She felt the same way about Jemmy so she could totally understand. With each passing day, she loved the white giraffe more.

Ben stopped in mid-sentence. 'Martine, look! Fresh rhino tracks, no more than an hour or two old. We must have just missed them.'

The two white rhinos were recent arrivals at Sawubona,

having been moved from a reserve on the Mozambique border where there was heavy poaching. Martine had been at Ben's house on the day they came and had seen them only once – in the distance and half-hidden by trees. There was something about their prehistoric form that made it hard to believe that they were real.

Martine wasn't sure how she felt about rhinos. She was passionate about saving and protecting all wild animals, but rhinos weren't exactly cuddly. Black rhinos had a reputation for being bad-tempered and white rhinos were short-sighted and clumsy. Both species looked as if they were wearing suits of armour and it was Martine's private opinion that if rhinos had a personality, it was well-hidden. Giraffes, on the other hand, were just plain wonderful.

When they reached the gate, Jemmy lowered himself to the ground so that she could hop off. Otherwise she'd have needed a ladder! Martine opened the gate and reached for the bag of carrots, apples and onions she'd left there earlier. While Shiloh guzzled two apples and a couple of Polo mints from Ben's pocket, Jemmy crunched his way through five carrots and four onions, juice dribbling down his chin, his eyes closed in ecstasy.

Martine breathed a contented sigh. 'Another day in paradise.'

They didn't notice Tendai until he was standing right in front of them. His powerful arms were folded across his chest and his dark face resembled a thundercloud. The scar on his cheek stood out like a bolt of lightning.

Even before he spoke, Martine knew what he was

going to say. She stifled a groan. Never mind the dishes, she and Ben were going to be doing Sawubona's worst chores for the next decade. At least.

That was the problem with living in paradise; trouble was rarely far behind.

· 2 ·

'Tendai, we were only having fun. I promise we won't ever do it again. Only please don't tell my grandmother. Pleeeaase,' begged Martine for the umpteenth time.

'Tell me what?' asked her grandmother, emerging from the kitchen in a flour-covered apron patterned with warthogs. The combined smells of French toast, caramelised fried bananas and homegrown mushrooms and tomatoes wafted after her. 'Anything interesting to report from the game reserve this morning? How did Shiloh and Jemmy get on? Do you think they're going to be friends? Come inside and give me all the news over breakfast. I don't want the food getting cold. See you later, Tendai. Don't forget to stop at the vet and pick up some ointment for that impala with the sore eye.'

Giving the children a look that said, 'This conversation is postponed but not forgotten,' Tendai jumped into his Land Rover. He revved the engine unnecessarily hard and bumped away down the drive. Martine and Ben sighed with relief. Pausing only to take off their boots and wash their hands at the kitchen sink, they hurried into the breakfast room. The French doors were open onto the garden. Sunlight spilled across the white tablecloth like liquid honey.

The cats, Warrior and Shelby, circled the table in hope of a treat. Beneath her stern exterior Gwyn Thomas was secretly a softy. It didn't take them long to persuade her to pour them a saucer of thick Jersey cream. Martine laughed at their blissed-out expressions.

Putting aside her worries about what Tendai might or might not say to her grandmother, she concentrated instead on trying to decide which was more delicious: a first course of freshly laid golden-yolked eggs fried with mushrooms and tomatoes, or a dessert course of French toast and fried banana with a dash of cream. Paw paw (papaya) juice accompanied the meal. Having vowed after the previous day's birthday feast never to eat again, Martine found to her surprise that she was able to fit in a New Year's Day breakfast with no difficulty.

Determined to keep her grandmother in a good mood, she kept up a stream of chatter. Between mouthfuls, she described the sunrise over the escarpment and the rhino tracks Ben had spotted beside the waterhole.

'Good to hear that the rhino are alive and well,' said Gwyn Thomas. 'Every visitor who called to book a ticket for this evening's Stars & Stripes safari seemed obsessed with seeing the Big Five. Our new rhino were top of the list. Of course, I tried my best to explain that there are hundreds of African animals every bit as special and exotic as elephant, lion, leopard, buffalo and rhino – white giraffes for one – but to no avail.'

'Maybe you should tell them the real reason why those particular animals are known as the Big Five,' suggested Martine.

'Because hunters consider them to be the most cunning and dangerous animals to kill? Yes, I was tempted to say that, but then I reminded myself that anyone visiting a game reserve must have an interest in wildlife. It's our job to inspire them and teach them to love and appreciate all creatures great and small as much as we do.'

Ben smiled. 'If you like, I can tell your guests about the Little Five: the Ant Lion, the Elephant Shrew, the Buffalo Weaver bird, the Leopard tortoise and the Rhinocerous beetle.'

'Oh, I adore Elephant shrews,' said Martine. 'They have this long curved nose like an elephant's trunk and are about the cutest thing you've ever seen.'

Her grandmother topped up their glasses with paw paw juice. 'Well, you'll have plenty of opportunity to wax lyrical about African wildlife this evening. We've sold eighteen tickets for the safari and barbecue. I'm relying on you both to help out wherever you can. It should be a

14

fun night. We have some fascinating guests coming. One or two of them are world famous.'

'World famous!' Martine practically bounced out of her chair with excitement. 'Who? Who's coming?'

Her grandmother zipped her lips. 'Can't say a word. It'll spoil the surprise.'

'Oh, please. It's hours until tonight and I won't be able to bear the suspense.'

'Anticipation will make it so much sweeter . . .'

'Can you give us a hint?'

The debate was interrupted when a vehicle came roaring up the drive. A door slammed and they heard the game warden's voice, deep and urgent. Gwyn Thomas frowned. 'That's strange. I thought Tendai was in a hurry to get to Storm Crossing. He must have forgotten something.'

The food in Martine's mouth turned to concrete. Clearly, Tendai had changed his mind and decided to tell her grandmother about their race sooner rather than later. Through the French doors, she could see Jemmy drinking from the waterhole, legs splayed, silver nose wrinkled. If she was banned from riding him, she'd be devastated. She glanced at Ben. He looked as worried as she did.

Tendai came rushing into the room, hat in his hands. 'Mrs Thomas, I'm sorry to interrupt, but the news is starting and you need to watch it.'

Martine was so preoccupied with the punishments likely coming her and Ben's way that for a moment she thought that they'd inadvertently ended up on the morning news. As the television flickered to life, she half-expected to see a video of the white giraffe and Basotho pony streaking across the reserve. Instead the anchorwoman intoned: 'Three black rhino were slaughtered by poachers at Leopard Rock game reserve in the Eastern Cape in the early hours of this morning.'

Gwyn Thomas was aghast. 'Our neighbours!'

'It was a savage attack that left one guard critically injured and brought the death toll of rhino in South Africa this year to 1,215. Conservation groups reacted with alarm to the latest outrage against this endangered species. Dr Marius Goss, head of the charity FAW, Fight for African Wildlife, describes the rhino-poaching crisis as an epidemic.'

The camera panned to Dr Goss, who looked out of place in the glass-and-chrome studio in his worn khaki clothes. His sunburned face was set with fury. He held up a tiny bottle. 'This bottle contains powdered rhino horn, which is made from a substance called keratin – no different to a human fingernail. And yet it is worth more than gold. Criminal gangs are selling it for $65,000 a kilogram to feed the demand from Asia, where many people believe it is a magical cure for everything from cancer and fevers, to blood disorders. The key word here is *magical*. It's make-believe. This stuff – ' he shook the bottle – 'is of no more value than your toenail clippings. It's precious to only one creature on earth – the rhino to whom it belongs.'

He leaned forward and stared directly into the camera. To Martine, it was as if he was appealing to her personally. 'Let me be clear. If we do not work together to halt this terrible trade, these gentle, smart, utterly unique animals, which have survived 50 million years of evolution, could be extinct within five years.'

The TV snapped off and a grim silence followed. Outside, a band of cloud had dulled the day.

Gwyn Thomas climbed slowly to her feet. 'Leopard Rock Reserve is two kilometres from here at most. The poachers might still be in the area. What's to stop them targeting Sawubona next? Never mind the expense, Tendai, we need to start rhino patrols as soon as possible.'

'I'll get onto it immediately, Mrs Thomas. I know a good man. If he's available, he could start next week.'

'That might be too late. I want the rhino guarded twenty-four seven, starting tonight. Ask Samson if he's willing to do the first watch. He's getting on a bit but he's experienced and he has a shotgun. And Tendai . . .?'

'Yes, Mrs Thomas.'

'The rhino aren't the only ones at risk. Remember that we're dealing with criminals who'll stop at nothing to get what they want, even if it means hurting the humans who get in their way. We all need to be extra vigilant. Martine and Ben, that includes you.'

Martine barely heard her. Her stomach was tying itself in knots. She almost wished that Tendai *had* come back to tell her grandmother about her race with Ben. Any punishment her grandmother could have meted out would have been preferable to this – the news that the animals she loved were once again threatened.

She thought about the ancient San cave paintings in

Sawubona's Secret Valley, a place known only to her, Ben and Grace, the *sangoma*. It was Grace who'd first shown Martine that her future was written on the cave walls. Recently, the paintings had revealed something else: that her life was inextricably bound to Ben's. They shared a destiny and a mission: to save and heal wild animals.

But a week earlier, a rock fall had sealed the cave forever. The walls had given up their last secret. Now if the hunters turned their sights on Sawubona, Martine and Ben would be walking blind.

3

It was when the helicopter landed on her grandmother's front lawn that Martine understood something extraordinary was happening. Something unreal. Something rather wonderful.

The shiny red door of the helicopter opened and five passengers exited in a swirl of grassy debris, crouching low to avoid the spinning blades. Gwyn Thomas said something but Martine didn't catch it above the deafening *thwup, thwup* of the engine. She raised her voice above the racket. 'Sorry, what did you say?'

'I can't hear you!' shouted her grandmother, cupping an ear. The rotors gave a final great swish and sprayed dust into Martine's eyes. Her world went dark.

'I don't believe it,' Ben said incredulously. 'Martine, look who it is.'

'I would if I could,' muttered Martine, eyes streaming. She rubbed her lids with her fists until she was finally able to make out a blurred image of her grandmother, Tendai and Ben greeting the visitors – a silver-haired man, a young woman and three teenage boys. There was something familiar about them.

Footsteps approached and her grandmother said: 'Martine, there's someone I'd like you to meet.'

Martine blinked owlishly. The boy before her swam into focus. He was about fifteen and wearing a tight black T-shirt and ripped blue jeans that matched the faded denim blue of his eyes. His haircut had been copied by millions of boys – and quite a few girls – across the world. She was dimly aware of Gwyn Thomas introducing him, but it wasn't necessary. His face was almost as familiar as her own.

Martine's mouth opened but all that came out was a squeak.

Accustomed to mute adoration, Jayden Lucas flashed a practised white smile and gripped her hand. 'A pleasure.'

To Martine's embarrassment, Gwyn Thomas said brightly: 'My granddaughter is your biggest fan, Jayden. There's a poster of your band on her bedroom wall. If you find yourself with a moment to spare this evening, perhaps you'd be kind enough to sign it for her?'

He bowed his dark head in response, showing off a miracle of styling.

Martine stammered, 'Jayden, I – uh, it's an honour to meet you. I l-love your music.'

What she really wanted to say was that it was Jayden's voice and the lyrics of his songs that had helped her through those first terrible months after her mum and dad died, when she'd believed herself friendless and alone. But she didn't because his gaze had drifted over her shoulder. He seemed tired. Or bored.

'Martine has a special gift,' Gwyn Thomas was saying. 'Actually, she has a couple of special gifts. One of them is riding a giraffe.'

Now they had his attention. He turned his blue gaze on her. 'For real? You can actually ride a giraffe? Maybe you could give me a demo—'

A shadow fell over them. Martine caught a whiff of cologne as an over-tanned man clapped a hand on the young singer's shoulder. She recognized him as Dirk Carswell, Jayden's manager. 'Excuse me, folks. Mind if I borrow our star for a photo opportunity? Gwyn, could I trouble you to join us? I'd like to ask you a few questions about tonight's itinerary.'

Martine hardly had time to draw breath before Tiffany, a PR girl in startlingly high heels, came over with Jayden's bandmates – drummer Liam Scott, short and cute with spiky blond hair, and guitarist Lachlan Avery, who had a fantastic chestnut quiff. Together with Jayden, they made up Take Flight, one of the hottest boy bands on the planet. Martine had heard that they were in concert in Cape Town and had begged to be allowed to go, but her grandmother had flatly refused on the grounds that it would be too expensive, too far and too noisy.

'You can close your mouth now,' teased Ben when Tiffany and the boys had departed in the direction of the house.

'Omigod,' said Martine. 'Am I hallucinating? Did Jayden Lucas just ask me to give him a demo of riding Jemmy?'

'That's only because he doesn't know that your famous white giraffe was beaten by a lowly Basotho pony this morning.'

'In your dreams,' scoffed Martine. 'As if Jayden's going to believe that a stumpy-legged pony could outrun a sleek and magnificent—'

'I doubt Jayden cares about anything except whether a single hair on his head is out of place. You could run a tractor on the amount of grease he puts in it.'

'It's wax,' said Martine, 'which you'd know if—'

She paused in mid-flow. An Aston Martin, a campervan decorated with cartoon cockatoos and a huge black SUV with blacked-out windows were pulling up the drive. While she was wasting time squabbling, interesting people were arriving and her favourite band were being entertained by people who couldn't possibly appreciate them as much as she did.

'How about we continue this debate later?' she suggested.

Ben grinned. 'Wouldn't miss it.'

They ran laughing across the lawn, slowing when they reached the house. In the driveway, the safari vehicles were being loaded with provisions for that evening's barbecue. The visitors had gathered on the verandah, where the table had been laid with drinks and snacks. The newest arrivals were Mr and Mrs Chan, a Chinese couple as short as they were round. They wore safari suits and dark glasses and stood silently nodding and smiling.

The VW campervan belonged to a party of five Australian surfers, who lit up the space with their sunny smiles and sea-salt bleached hair. Also present were John and Olivia Johnson, both doctors from Cheshire, England, and two Belgian businessmen called Lars and Kobe.

While Ben went in search of soft drinks, Martine leaned awkwardly against the wall. She stole glance at the Take Flight boys. Liam and Lachlan were posing for photos with the Australians. Jayden was nowhere to be seen.

She was debating whether to nip upstairs to fetch her poster for him to sign when she spotted him. He and his manager were standing in the shadows of the mango trees some distance from the house. Judging from their body language, they were having a row.

Ben reappeared with two glasses of fizzy red grape juice, decorated with raspberries and twirly zebra-striped straws. Nearby, the Belgians were chatting to the doctors.

'We are in ze mobile phone business,' said Lars, 'but zat is not our real passion.'

'And what's that?' asked John Johnson.

Lars beamed. 'Perhaps you will not approve. We love hunting.' He threw up his hands with glee. 'In Europe we have many trophies in our homes. I myself recently shot a brown bear in Transylvania.'

Martine bit back a squeak of horror.

'How could you?' cried Olivia Johnson. 'What gives you the right to steal the life of such a beautiful creature?'

'Please, Madam, don't be upset. Zese bears are quite common in Romania and other parts of ze Continent. Zey are not endangered. But never before have we seen ze wild enimals of Africa. We hef our sights set on the Big Five. Don't worry, we can't afford the hunting license for anything better than a buffalo. No leopard or elephant for us. For a rhino head, we would hef to win the lottery.'

'Or rob a bank,' joked Kobe.

Martine was ready to explode with rage. Ben gripped her arm warningly. 'Remember what your grandmother said. Not everyone who comes to Sawubona cares about wildlife. It's up to us to show them what they're missing.'

She knew he was right. All the ranting in the world wouldn't change the minds of the hunters. The best that she and Ben could hope for was that experiencing African wildlife at its most primal might inspire some guests to think differently. 'The African bush is some powerful *muti*,' Grace liked to say. 'Once it's in your blood it will haunt you forever.'

Martine believed the same was true of wild animals. That given the chance to look deep into the eyes of a lion or elephant and see the untamed, magnificent spirit who lived there, few people could remain unchanged.

As if to prove Ben's point about the lesser-known animals being special too, Gwyn Thomas emerged from the house with a galago on her shoulder. He was all eyes and mouse-like ears. She introduced him as Echo, a bush baby orphan being hand-reared by Samson in Sawubona's little wildlife hospital. Inquisitive and affectionate, he would, if left to his own devices, sneak into the kitchen and gobble anything he could get his paws on, from marmalade to prawns.

Someone tapped the rim of a glass with a spoon. The hubbub died away. Jayden had rejoined the group, but was visibly agitated. On the opposite side of the verandah, Dirk Carswell wore a fixed smile.

'A very warm welcome to our Stars and Stripes safari, so-called because later you'll be dining beneath the stars, and because at least some of the animals you'll spot today are striped.

'Many of you have expressed interest in seeing the Big Five: lion, leopard, elephant, buffalo and, of course, rhino. Here at Sawubona we adore animals of all shapes and sizes and we're going to do our best to show you why our other creatures matter too. We also like our wildlife to have the freedom to come and go as they please. Try not to be disappointed if their choice this evening is to hide in the undergrowth rather than roll on their backs to provide you with cute photographs to show your friends.'

Everyone laughed.

'But don't worry. Our guides are among the best in the business. Over the next few hours, we'll be explaining why we're passionate about conserving wild animals, who ask nothing of humans but to be left alone to be free

25

to roam, eat good food and love their families just as we love ours.'

She handed a grape to Echo, who squeaked with delight. 'Now if my ears aren't deceiving me, our last guests have arrived.'

Around the corner came a woman so exquisite that the chatter on the verandah died, as if someone had switched off a radio. She was wearing a long-sleeved jade silk tunic over billowing white silk trousers and her limbs were as delicate as any fawn's. Glossy black hair framed her face. When she reached the verandah steps, she didn't so much climb them as float.

A sallow-skinned man, bursting out of his shirt, waddled in her wake. He leaned heavily on a stick. The phrase 'Beauty and the Beast' came into Martine's mind.

Gwyn Thomas greeted them warmly and turned to the spellbound company. 'Please join me in welcoming another honoured guest to Sawubona. Meet An Nzuyen and her uncle, Huynh. An is Vietnam's most revered ballerina. Now that we are all here, our safari can begin. Kindly make your way to the two safari vehicles out front.'

'Stars beneath the stars,' Ben murmured to Martine. 'This should be a night to remember. Hope it's for all the right reasons.'

4

'Are we going to die?' asked Liam. He clutched at the guardrail as a young bull elephant mock-charged the Land Rover, pulling up barely a metre away. Dust roiled up around the beast in a burnt-orange cloud. He stood outlined against the sunset, flapping his ears furiously.

'Don't be so soft,' said Lachlan, who was filming the incident on his phone. 'We're in a massive, solid vehicle. What's he gonna do – tip us over? Climb onto the back and squash us?'

Tiffany paled. 'Don't. I can just see the headlines now: TAKE FLIGHT STARS GORED IN JUMBO HORROR.

Martine clung to her seat as Tendai made as much noise as possible – revving the engine, banging the side of his door and yelling at Kato – while reversing slowly away. She didn't tell Liam he had every reason to be frightened. That Kato, a teenage bull with attitude, had become increasingly arrogant in recent months. Whenever he saw the Land Rover he reacted aggressively. The rangers had had several close calls trying to escape him. She thought it best not to mention that Kato was more than capable of flipping over the vehicle, crushing it and killing them. Sometimes ignorance was bliss, especially since on this occasion Kato quit after he'd done his best to scare them.

'I was *kidding*,' Liam insisted when the danger was past. 'Of course I knew he was only having a game. Good adrenalin rush, though, and great for our website, hey, Tiff?'

Tiffany giggled nervously. She had a dream job, but it wasn't an easy one. Keeping high-energy, high-maintenance teen superstars out of trouble and out of the tabloids was a round-the-clock mission. Earlier, Gwyn Thomas had received a call from the guard at the main gate to say that two carloads of Take Flight groupies had tried to bribe him to let them into the reserve. When he'd refused, some of the girls had become quite hysterical. The police had almost been called.

'If that elephant's a menace to visitors, maybe your grandmother should get rid of him,' was Dirk Carswell's sour comment.

Martine hid a scowl. While waiting to board the safari vehicles she'd overheard Jayden say in a low voice to his manager: 'You need to fix what you've done before it's too late, Dirk. If you don't, *I* will.'

'Watch yourself, kiddo,' Carswell had warned. 'Your fifteen seconds of fame is almost up.'

She had no idea what had fuelled their row, but she was quite sure that it was Carswell's fault. How dare he threaten Jayden like that? Wasn't it the role of a boy band's manager to protect his young charges, not bully them?

'Kato's only gone off the rails because there's no older bull in the herd to put him in his place,' she told him now, forcing a smile. 'He needs a patriarch – a father figure – to teach him some respect.'

Carswell laughed. 'You hear that boys? When young bulls go off the rails, they need a patriarch to teach them some respect.'

There followed lots of joshing from Liam and Lachlan. Whatever her opinion of the manager, it was obvious to Martine that he had a good relationship with at least two of the band members. Only Jayden stayed silent.

Martine was glad that Ben was travelling in the second Land Rover so he could help Thomas, the new ranger, answer questions from the guests. It meant that she could study her idol without Ben rolling his eyes. 'Why don't you ask him if he walks on water?' he'd teased at the house.

At the beginning of the game drive, the young singer had sat stiff and tense in his seat, his dark hair curling over the collar of his black T-shirt. He'd spent more time checking his iPhone than he had watching out for wildlife. Then Tendai braked to allow a family of warthogs to cross the road. To Martine's surprise, Jayden had burst out laughing at the sight of the hairy piglets.

'They're so ugly they're almost beautiful,' he said as they'd scampered away in single file, tails pointing skyward like aerials.

After that, he'd relaxed. The flaming sunset and soul-soothing peace of the bush had worked its magic on him as it did every day with Martine. He'd gazed in awe at the cheetahs sitting regally on an anthill on the plain. He'd shivered with delight when a lion roared unexpectedly. Unlike some of the other guests, he and Olivia Johnson had taken great interest in some of the lesser creatures Tendai pointed out – guinea-fowl with nodding blue heads, two shiny dung beetles and a mongoose on the hunt for a juicy cobra.

Tendai's radio crackled. He spoke into it and, at the next side road, turned right. They bumped along until they reached a bridge. Switching off the engine, he put a finger to his lips and pointed. There was a whisper of clothing and the soft squeak of leather seats as all the guests turned at once. Two rhinos watched them from a grove of trees.

'Meet Spartacus and Cleo,' Tendai said proudly.

Martine leaned forward so she could see past Tiffany and the Chans. Spartacus and Cleo were white rhinos, simple to identify because they had a wide mouth for grazing. Black rhinos were smaller and had a pointed lip for browsing bushes and shrubs.

Tendai explained that when nineteenth-century Dutch

settlers first encountered rhino in South Africa, they called them *weit*, meaning wide, rhino. The English misheard it as 'white' rhino and the label stuck, despite the fact that both species are grey. 'The other main difference is temperament. Black rhino are aggressive and quick to anger.'

'These white rhinos look as if they're wearing suits of armour, like knights of the realm,' said Olivia Johnson. 'No wonder they get poached. I can't imagine they run very fast.'

'You're wrong about that,' said Tendai. 'At full charge, a rhino can reach 55 kilometres per hour – faster than a racehorse but slow compared to a springbok, which can clock up 100 kilometres per hour. Springbok and cheetahs are the Ferraris of the bush.'

'A rhino could outrun Seabiscuit?'

'Theoretically, but only over a short distance. They can also change direction faster than a top class polo pony. No ranger ever approaches a rhino without first deciding which tree he or she is going to climb if it all goes wrong. The white rhino weighs well over five tons. You wouldn't want to be trampled by one.'

'Maybe that's why the collective noun for rhinos is a crash,' said Martine, flushing shyly when everyone laughed, including Jayden.

'They're smart too,' Tendai went on. 'When a rhino sleeps beneath a tree it will always position itself so that its spine is aligned with the branch that throws the largest shadow. From a distance, that makes it invisible.'

'Not invisible enough, sadly,' said John Johnson. 'We

31

heard the news report about those poor rhinos on your neighbouring reserve. What are you doing to keep these ones safe? Would they be safer if you cut off their horns?'

'No, they would not. It's an expensive and risky operation for everyone concerned and it doesn't help. Worse, it leaves the rhino partially disabled. For rhino, a horn is not just a means of defence. It's a multi-purpose tool they use to dig up bulbs and termites, turn over logs, hook down branches or take bark off trees, especially in times of drought. It's as important to them as your hands are to you. Besides, a poacher won't spare a rhino just because it has no horn. He'll either kill it so he doesn't waste his time tracking it on another night, or he'll kill it and cut out the section of horn that lies beneath the skull, often while the rhino is still alive.'

'How about poisoning the buyers?' Liam suggested dramatically. 'If rhino horns were injected with arsenic or cyanide, it would soon stop people buying them to cure cancer or get rid of bunions or whatever crazy idea they have.'

'That would be illegal,' cried Mr Chan, speaking for first time since they'd left the house. 'A person who is sick and who uses the poisoned horn because it is their only hope of getting cured might get more ill or perish. This would be terrible.'

Martine eyed him curiously. Although he and his wife had smiled and nodded through the game drive so far, they'd seemed far away, their eyes glazed over. It was as if they were there but not really there. Until they saw the rhino. Now they were wide awake.

'If there are people in this world idiotic enough or superstitious enough to believe that a substance no different to my nails is going to cure cancer, it's hardly surprising that others are scrambling to make a fast buck out of them,' said Mick, one of the surfers. 'Two or three rhino horns would fund many years of surfing and chilling. I could quit my job and pretty much live at the beach.'

'Whoo-hoo! Happy days!' laughed his mate. 'Don't tempt me.'

A muscle worked in Tendai's cheek. He continued as if they hadn't spoken.

'Poisoning the horn would be against the law,' he told Liam. 'We could be sued if someone "perished", as Mr Chan put it, even if they did so swallowing horn obtained in a country where poaching rhino is a criminal act. No, the best thing we can do for rhino is convince people they're worth saving.'

'There's your problem right there,' said Carswell. 'Rhinos aren't dazzling like leopards or cuddly like pandas or lion cubs. Not enough people care about saving them.'

Kobe slapped his knee. 'Exactly! Zey are not loveable.'

'That's only because you don't know or understand them,' said Tendai. 'If you or anyone else would like to come with me see these rhino at close range, you will soon see that there are few animals in the world more worthy of being preserved. Rhino are uniquely wonderful and I can prove it.'

He stared challengingly at the manager, but Dirk picked

up his camera and trained its long lens on Spartacus and Cleo. Tendai turned his attention to the band. 'Any of you boys up for it? You never know, it might be a life-changing experience.'

Tiffany was horrified. 'Our insurers would have a fit. If the Take Flight boys were attacked by rampaging five-ton rhinos, there's no way they'd pay out. Even if the boys were only scratched it would be a disaster. Their gorgeous faces and bodies are their fortune.'

'What about our music?' Jayden asked wryly. 'Doesn't that count?'

'Well, yes, but it also helps that you look the way you do.'

Liam preened and ran his fingers through his blond spikes. Lachlan put up a token protest, but soon backed down when Dirk agreed with Tiffany's comments. Jayden said nothing. He had his phone in his hand again and was sullenly checking messages. Martine's opinion of him took a dive. Ben had been right. He was nothing but a spoiled, pampered pop brat.

'*We'll* come with you, Tendai,' the Johnsons said firmly, picking up their cameras and clambering off the high back of the safari Land Rover.

Martine stood up. 'So will I.'

Tendai went over to the other vehicle and repeated his offer. They were joined by Ben, a couple of surfers and, to everyone's astonishment, An, the ballerina, unsuitably attired in her *oa dai*, Vietnamese traditional dress.

Tendai slung his rifle over his shoulder. 'Stay low, stay quiet and do exactly what I say. Everyone ready?'

'Not quite,' said Olivia.

A row had broken out on the back of the Land Rover. Carswell's voice rose. 'Don't you dare disobey me, Jayden. You're going nowhere. I absolutely forbid it.'

Jayden said bitterly: 'You don't own me, Dirk. You can't control me.'

He swung off the vehicle and jogged over to them, his sunglasses hiding his expression. 'Sorry to keep you waiting. Sometimes in the business I'm in, I forget to think for myself.'

Olivia gave him a warm smile. 'Now, Tendai, we're ready to go.'

'Wait,' said Ben. 'There's one more.'

Lars, the Belgian bear-hunter, materialised out of a plume of dust left by the other Land Rover. He was standing on the sandy track, one hand raised. 'May I join you?'

'Great,' Martine murmured in disgust. 'He wants to size up another head for his living-room wall.'

Tendai flipped the safety catch off on his rifle. 'I believe we're finally good to go. Remember what I said: stay low, stay quiet and choose the tree you're going to climb in the event of an emergency. A game reserve is not Disneyland and rhino are not toys. Make a mistake and you'll pay with your life.'

· 5 ·

When they were close enough to the rhinos to see the frayed edges of their ears, Tendai turned with a smile. 'I have something very special to show you. I didn't want to say anything before now because if too many others had joined us we wouldn't have been able to come. You are the lucky ones.'

'Well, that's nice to hear,' John Johnson said. 'Are you going to tell us what it is?'

'Follow me and you'll see it for yourself.'

They crept through the bush towards Spartacus and Cleo. The immense animals shifted to face the possible threat, as light on their feet as dancers. They blinked and sniffed the air. Rhinos were short-sighted and Martine's grandmother always claimed that, at thirty metres, they could barely tell a person from a tree. However, these rhinos were clearly wearing contact lenses. They looked ready to pound the intruders into pancakes at a second's notice.

Tendai indicated a long sloping boulder. 'We wait here. Sit down or lie down and be as still as possible.'

Martine found herself lying between Ben and Jayden in a sort of nature boy-pop idol sandwich. It was unnerving. Still, she smiled to herself when she saw how, in this setting, Ben came into his own. His worn olive green cargo trousers, khaki T-shirt and dusty desert boots were infinitely more suited to bushwalking than Jayden's ripped jeans, studded belt and hi-tech trainers.

But it was about so much more than their clothing. Ben was totally in tune with his surroundings. He moved silently, missed nothing and could read 'sign' – the rangers' word for the traces an animal makes when it passes – as easily as most people read books. Tendai had once told her that tracking was a rare gift. You were either born with it or you weren't. Some skills could be learned but unless a person could think themselves into an animal's head, they'd never make a great tracker.

'Oh, my goodness!' exclaimed Olivia.

The rhinos had shifted apart. Cleo's gaze was fixed on the shifting shadows behind her. There was a series of mouse-like squeaks, then a baby rhino shot from between the flanks of its parents.

Martine had only lived at Sawubona a year and there

were still gaps in her wildlife knowledge. Rhino calves were among them. It was only now she realized that she'd never actually seen a picture of a rhino baby. If she'd thought of them at all, she'd imagined them as miniature versions of their parents.

Nothing had prepared her for the 70 kilograms of armour-plated cuteness that came barrelling their way. His legs were too short, his lily-shaped ears too big, his eyes too small and his skin so loose and bulky it looked like a hand-me-down from an older brother. It was as if ET had been merged with the sweetest prehistoric monster imaginable.

For Martine, it was love at first sight. Judging by the delighted laughter that greeted his appearance, she wasn't alone.

When the calf caught sight of the visitors, he bounced to a stop with a comical look of surprise. Instead of retreating to the safety of his mum's side he tottered closer. His mother lumbered after him. She lowered her horn threateningly and puffed with agitation.

An gave a small scream. Martine grabbed Ben and Jayden's arms in fright. Her life was over! She was going to be trampled into the dirt before she could get to her chosen tree. She'd never again race Jemmy against Shiloh and Ben. Jayden would never sing another note. Tendai cocked his rifle and took aim at Cleo. The calf rushed headlong in their direction, skidding to a stop just metres away. Fortunately, his mum did too.

Martine forgot to breathe. Was she dreaming or was the rhino baby staring directly at her? Before she could be sure, he began to play. Round and round he raced, like an exhuberant puppy. His mum watched indulgently. Her great head, weighed down by one and a half metres of horn, swung to follow his progress.

Martine had the odd sensation of being drawn into the warm brown depths of the rhino's eyes. The spirit that resided in them was gentle, intelligent and vulnerable, but the quality that blazed most strongly was love. The rhino mum adored her baby as much as Martine's mum had once adored her.

A tear ran down Martine's cheek. She was embarrassed to be overcome with emotion when she was squeezed between two boys, one of whom was her musical hero. But she needn't have worried. Ben was overwhelmed and even Jayden had given up being cool. There was a huge grin on his face.

Worn out from its exertions, the rhino baby flopped to the ground. It was asleep almost instantly. Cleo sank down beside him. She shut her eyes, her long black lashes spiky against her leathery skin.

'She is paying us a compliment,' Tendai said in a low voice. 'This is her way of telling us that she trusts us not to harm her calf.'

'What's the baby's name?' asked Martine.

'He doesn't have one yet. He's only a few days old. If you think of something, let me know.'

Tendai motioned for them to return to the Land Rover. Night was falling and the first stars were scattered across a peacock-blue sky streaked with gold.

Nobody spoke on the drive to the escarpment. Martine

wished that she could read the thoughts of the visitors –
of Jayden, whose face was in shadow, or Lars the hunter,
who seemed to be waging some inner war with himself.
An, the Vietnamese ballerina, was present only in body.
She stared out at the dark game reserve as they drove, her
face sad. Only the surfers and the Johnsons were smiling.

High on the escarpment where Martine and Ben had begun their race early that morning, a long table had been decorated with a white cloth, velvety pink proteas and blue Agapanthas. Cutlery and glasses sparkled in the flickering light of lanterns made from gourds.

Unusually for the Eastern Cape, it was a balmy night. Frogs, cicadas and an owl serenaded the guests as they ate a Cape Malay curry (chicken for the meat-eaters and a vegetarian version with apricots for Martine, her grandmother and Ben), plus barbecued corn, fish kebabs and saffron rice. With the exception of Liam, who kept telling everyone that he was a 'burger and fries man' and didn't do 'exotic food', the meal was a hit with the guests.

Martine had engineered it so that she was beside Tiffany, only two seats away from the Take Flight boys. She would have liked Ben to sit next to her too, but he'd insisted on being at the far end of the table, near the surfers.

'I don't understand what your problem is,' Martine said crossly. 'Liam and Lachlan are very nice and Jayden's a dream. He's soooo lovely.'

'I'm sure they're just peachy but I prefer real people.'

'Who are you to judge them?' said Martine, her temper flaring. 'You don't even know them.'

'And you do?'

'Actually, I've got to know them extremely well over the past few hours. Anyway, you're just jealous,' she accused.

'Why would I be jealous?'

'Because they're rich and famous and supremely talented. Have you any idea how many millions of people would give anything to trade places with us this evening?'

'Okay, now I know you've lost your mind,' said Ben. 'When you find it, I'll be at the other end of the table.'

Had Martine not been in a state of euphoria induced by the encounter with the baby rhino and the mind-blowing fact that she was dining with one of the biggest boy bands on the planet, Ben's attitude would have upset her. They'd only ever had one real row and it had distressed Martine so much that she'd vowed it would never happen again. But she was too busy enjoying herself to let it get to her.

Dirk Carswell was seated beside An Nzuyen and her odd uncle. An's mouth was smiling but her body language was tense. At one point she seemed to snap at her uncle. Whatever she said amused Dirk. He and Uncle Huynh got up from the table and moved off to the dark fringes of the barbecue for a smoke. Martine was surprised. She couldn't imagine what the men had in common.

Putting it out of her mind, she settled down to listen as the Take Flight boys chatted and teased one another about their adventures on the road. There'd been a hair-raising flight on their private jet during a storm, and a crazed fan who abseiled down from the tenth floor of a hotel in a bid to climb through the window of their suite on the floor below. Next they were off to Paris, the final stop on their thirty-five date tour.

'Dirk, can we have it in our contract that we're to have a constant supply of burgers and *pommes frites* in Paris?' Liam called down the table. 'Plus that hot chocolate that's so thick you can eat it with a knife and fork?'

'Sure thing,' his manager replied distractedly.

'*You* can have that,' said Lachlan. 'I want big platters of smelly *fromage* and baguettes. And snails. I think I'll try snails and maybe a few frogs legs with garlic.'

'Urgh,' said Martine.

Jayden laughed. 'Just kidding. Enough about us. We saw pretty much every animal on the reserve today, Maria, but we didn't see your white giraffe. Any chance you can call him? We'd love to meet him.'

The hurt that Martine felt because he'd forgotten her name was partly offset by the thrill that he wanted to meet Jemmy. 'It's Martine,' she corrected him.

'What's Martine?'

'My name. It's Martine.' She went on hastily: 'Jemmy's quite shy but I'll see what I can do. We'll need to walk to the edge of the escarpment. He won't come here because there are too many people.'

'I'll stay and keep Tiffany company,' mumbled Liam through a mouthful of pudding. He'd decided that milk tart and *koeksisters,* which were syrup-drenched twists of deep-fried dough, met his requirements for calorie-laden food.

'And I'll be along in a bit,' said Lachlan. 'First, I want to talk to that fabulous Vietnamese dancer.'

Olivia Johnson leaned over. 'I couldn't help overhearing your conversation, Martine. Are you really going to call your white giraffe? Mind if I come too?'

Martine tried to catch Ben's eye as she, Jayden and Olivia left the table, but he was watching Mr Chan, who was talking animatedly to Tendai. He and his wife were leaving early because Mrs Chan had a migraine. Thomas, the new ranger, was taking them back to their hotel.

While Jayden fiddled with his phone's fancy camera settings and Olivia tried to identify a night bird, Martine discreetly blew on her silent dog whistle. It was inaudible to the human ear but dogs and giraffes could hear it from enormous distances. If Jemmy was within range he'd come running.

Waiting on the edge of the treeline with Jayden and Olivia, Martine reviewed the events of the day in her head. What a story she'd have to tell the teenagers at her new school. 'Jayden and I had the best time hanging out with my white giraffe . . .' she'd begin. 'Yes, I mean Jayden Lucas from Take Flight. Didn't I mention that we're friends? He just adores wildlife, you know. When the Take Flight boys visited Sawubona, me and Jayden spent ages watching a baby rhino play . . .'

As if reading her thoughts, Jayden asked: 'What's the name of the place where we saw the rhinos?'

Martine jumped guiltily. 'Uh, it doesn't really have a name. Wildlife reserves don't work that way. None of the roads have signs. We tend to identify places because they have a burned tree or an anthill shaped like a castle. One of my favourite corners of Sawubona has a boulder that resembles a sleeping lion.'

A look of impatience flitted across Jayden's face. He raked a hand through his dark hair. 'In that case, surely you could do the same with the spot where we saw the rhinos? It would be great if I could describe it if I'm being interviewed for a magazine or posting something on social media. Watching the rhino baby play was one of the greatest experiences of my life – as good as performing live at the O2 Arena.'

Martine glowed at the thought of him telling reporters about the wonders of Sawubona. Maybe the reserve would get a sudden influx of tourists – not something she particularly wanted, but it would bring in extra money for her grandmother.

'The rhinos were close to Troll Bridge on the Rooibos River,' she said. 'That's not the actual name of the bridge. My grandmother just calls it that because it's the sort of darkly magical place where trolls might lurk.'

He laughed. 'That's fantastic. What a great image. Maybe I'll Tweet about it later.'

Martine went cold. 'There's no way you can put it on Twitter. What if a poacher sees it? You'll have given away the rhinos' location.'

His smile would have charmed a charging rhino, but his patronising tone told her she was being paranoid. 'We have millions of fans on Twitter, but I'm willing to bet that not one of them is a gun-toting wildlife criminal. Most are sweet kids like you.'

'I don't mean to butt in, but I think Martine is right to be cautious given the recent poaching at Leopard Rock Reserve,' interjected Olivia. 'Anyway, I really don't understand this incessant need of young people to update strangers on their every waking moment. Isn't it enough to share your life with family and real friends?'

'It's not about that,' Jayden said defensively. 'Me, Liam and Lachlan want our fans to share in our success. We want to engage with them, not keep them at a distance like we're too good for them.'

Over by the fire, an African band began to play. A couple of surfers got up to dance, followed by Liam and Tiffany. The drums beat faster and faster. Martine's heart pounded in anxious rhythm. Just as she was beginning to think that the music had frightened away the white giraffe, there was a swish of branches. Jemmy strolled out of the trees, his head silhouetted against the moon. Martine felt a surge of love and pride. Always nervous around strangers, the white giraffe was hesitant about approaching, but he did linger long enough for the visitors to stroke his silver nose.

Jayden and Olivia were smitten. The tension that had crept into the group dissolved.

'He's awesome, Martine,' said Jayden. 'Can you really ride him? How do you get up there – a crane? Sorry about getting your name wrong earlier by the way. I must have misheard when we were introduced. It's a hazard of being a musician: deafness. Let me make it up to you. How 'bout we take a giraffe selfie?'

By the time the Stars and Stripes safari was over, there'd been so many highlights that it was hard to choose between them. For Martine, two stood out. An Nzuyen performing a haunting dance was one of them.

But Martine knew she'd remember forever the moment when the Take Flight boys performed their biggest hit, 'Firefly Summer', borrowing the instruments of the local musicians. With Liam on African drums, Lachlan on a homemade guitar and Jayden's soulful voice filling the night, they demonstrated with ease why they'd won the hearts of millions. By the time they'd finished, there wasn't a dry eye on the reserve. Even Ben was impressed.

'Today's been pretty special for us,' Jayden had told his audience, the smallest he'd played to since Dirk discovered him busking on a street corner in Exeter, Devon. 'Some day I'll write a song about it.'

Minutes later, the band was gone, taking flight in their red helicopter and spinning away into the darkness. The remaining guests and Ben had left shortly afterwards. Had it not been for the giraffe selfie on her phone, which brought a smile to Martine's face every time she looked at it, the whole amazing day might have been a dream.

Martine woke with a sudden, violent start. There was a sick feeling in her stomach – not the kind of nausea that comes from eating bad food but the kind that accompanies guilt. She'd said or done something that was going come back to haunt her. If only she could remember what it was.

It was two twenty-one a.m. on her bedside clock. She sat up, bleary-eyed. When she pushed aside the curtain, the black cloth of night glittered with stars. One lonely evening, not long after arriving in Africa, she'd looked out of her window during a fierce storm and glimpsed the white giraffe illuminated by lightning. Desperate for a friend, Martine had crept out into the rainy darkness to find an animal that everyone insisted existed only in myth. Looking back she still shuddered at the risk she'd taken, but it had been worth it to meet Jemmy, the best thing that had ever happened to her.

So strong was the memory that she stared for a long time into the blackness, willing him to appear, but there was no movement down at the waterhole. Still feeling unwell, Martine decided to go downstairs for a drink. As she passed the window on the landing, she noticed a light circling in the distance. In her half-asleep state, she thought it was a UFO.

Looking again, she realised it was a helicopter. Immediately, her imagination went into overdrive. A miracle had occurred! The Take Flight boys were on their way back to Sawubona! One of them had forgotten something important – a passport or a sheet of song lyrics dropped down the side of a Land Rover seat. They'd arrive full of apologies for waking the house at such an ungodly hour. By the time they'd found whatever it was that was lost, dawn would be breaking. Her grandmother would offer them breakfast. Jayden would get to sign Martine's poster after all. They could hang out with Jemmy again.

The light shrank to a pinprick then disappeared.

Down in the kitchen, Martine smiled to herself. What a muppet she was. Even if one of the band members had forgotten something they certainly wouldn't be returning in person to collect it. They needed their beauty sleep. They'd send an emissary: Dirk, or Tiffany in her spiky stilettoes.

She had the fridge open and was drinking passion-fruit juice from the carton when she suddenly choked. Panic swept through her. A helicopter circling the game reserve at night could mean only one thing.

'Grandmother!' she screamed, sprinting for the stairs. 'Grandmother, wake up!'

Racing onto the landing she saw the light again. It rose as she watched and swooped away to the north.

Gwyn Thomas's bedroom door crashed open and she rushed out, tying her robe. 'What is it, Martine? Are you ill? Is there a burglar?'

'I think I saw a helicopter land in the reserve ... ' Martine began, but before she could get any further, the phone rang.

Her grandmother rushed to pick it up. Martine could hear her muffled voice. 'Yes, Samson? NO! Oh no. And the little one? What about you? Don't move. We're on our way.'

The phone was slammed down. When her grandmother reappeared, she seemed to have aged ten years.

'It's the rhinos, isn't it?' cried Martine. 'The poachers have attacked them. Are they dead or alive?'

'Martine, you were right to wake me. There's an emergency in the reserve. Yes, it involves the rhino. I can't risk leaving you here on your own. You're to come with me but you'll have to stay in the vehicle. Is that understood?'

'But maybe I can help.'

'No!' Gwyn Thomas said harshly. 'Not this time. You're to stay in the vehicle with the doors locked and that's final.'

The night wind was a shard of ice, slashing at Martine's face. She braced herself against the dashboard, but Tendai drove so fast and with such fury that there was no way to prevent being flung from side to side or bounced up and down. Normally, her grandmother would have admonished him, but this was a matter of life and death. The vet had been called and would be with them within the hour. By then it would almost certainly be too late.

They rounded a bend at speed, another thing Tendai would never do under normal circumstances in case an animal was crossing the road. Samson was sitting on a boulder, holding a rag to a cut on his temple. His trousers were streaked with blood. Tendai skidded to a halt beside him. He leaped out, rifle in hand. Samson gestured into the bush with a torch. Pausing only to utter a few words of comfort to his friend, the game warden took a path through the long grass. Darkness closed behind him like a curtain.

Gwyn Thomas was at Samson's side with a first aid kit. The old man swallowed a couple of pain-killers and allowed her to dress his cut, but refused any other assistance. His only concern was the rhinos.

'I'm so sorry, *Gogo*,' he said over and over, using the African term of endearment for all grandmothers. 'I'm so sorry.'

'Samson, what's happened tonight is not your fault. The people who did this weren't amateurs. This was a military operation, planned to the last detail. Most likely it's the same gang who wreaked havoc at Leopard Rock Reserve. Some nerve, they have, striking again when the police are combing the area for them. I'm only thankful you weren't killed.

'Now Tendai and I need to do what we can for the rhino. Stay here with Martine. You can take care of each other. The vet and police should arrive at any moment. When they do, point them in our direction, don't bring them. Neither of you are to leave the vehicle. That's an order.'

After she'd gone, a spooky silence descended. Sensing danger, the night creatures had stopped their music. Martine was desperate to know what had happened, but she didn't want to stress Samson further. Finally, she said: 'Are the pills helping your sore head?'

'No, but I deserve much worse. Whatever your grandmother says, I failed in my duty. At first when I saw the helicopter, I thought it might be the young musicians returning. I didn't realize that the rhino had been shot with a tranquiliser dart until they crumpled to the ground. I messaged Tendai right away and ran to find the helicopter. Next thing, the sky landed on my head. That's how it felt. When I regained consciousness, the poachers were gone and the ground beside the Rooibos River was like something from a battlefield . . . Oh, Martine, I hope you never have to hear a rhino calf cry.'

The sick feeling that had woken Martine intensified. A hideous thought gnawed at the fringes of her mind, but she pushed it away.

'Don't you dare blame yourself, Samson. Like my grandmother said, this was planned. You don't just fly over a game reserve in the dark and get lucky finding a rhino. It would be easier landing a tennis ball on the moon.'

An unearthly cry ripped through the darkness. It was as if all the pain and anguish of every rhino that had ever been tormented by humans was concentrated in that one sound. Martine flung open the door and jumped out.

Samson managed to grab the hem of her jacket. 'No, Martine. There's a reason your *gogo* told you to stay in the car. What's happened tonight is something a child should never see.'

'I have to go. I might be able to help.'

'Little one, there is nothing anyone can do.'

'You don't know that.'

Martine twisted out of her jacket and bolted away down the narrow dark path, tripping and stumbling. Thorns and grass with razor-edges slashed at her neck and bare forearms. Fine roots ensnared her boots. She could hear Samson calling, but he was limping and she knew he'd never catch her.

A shot rang out. Martine's heart and legs seized up. She crouched and covered her head with her hands, as if her palms could stop a bullet. When there were no further shots, she sprinted on, crossing Troll Bridge and bursting into the clearing.

Tendai and her grandmother looked round in horror. The butt of Tendai's rifle was still smoking. He was standing over Spartacus, wiping his eyes.

Gwyn Thomas was trying to comfort the mother rhino. Hours earlier Cleo had watched her baby son play, her expression full of love. Now she lay moaning in a pool of crimson. Her horn was gone, hacked off her living body with an axe. Her gentle, wise face was a bloody ruin. She was unconscious but surfacing slowly to a world of agony.

Her bewildered calf took two steps forward before retreating at speed. He was terrified to be near her and even more afraid to be away from the mum who had been the centre of his universe. His panicked, desperate squeaks as he pleaded with her to rescue him and take him to safety tore at Martine's heart. She wished she could hold him in her arms.

'Martine, you should not be here,' cried her grandmother, struggling to her feet. 'I told you to stay away.'

She grabbed Martine by the shoulders and pulled her away. 'I'm sorry you've had to witness this tragic scene, but I'm also livid that you disobeyed me. What if the bullet Tendai fired had ricocheted and hit you? What if you'd run into one of the poachers? We're going back to the vehicle immediately.'

Martine ducked under her arm. Evading her grandmother's grasp, she kneeled down and put a hand on Cleo's head. Rage swept through her like a forest fire. Gwyn Thomas's lips were moving and she was tugging at Martine's arm but Martine was immoveable. She could neither hear, nor did she care what her grandmother was saying. She placed her hands on either side of the bloody hole on Cleo's face. They grew hotter and hotter.

Her vision misted over. She could hear the drumbeats of the ancients, see a blazing fire and feel energy flowing through her with the force of a river in flood. Beneath her fingers, the wound almost sizzled.

The rhino's eye snapped open. There was something accusing in her stare. Martine had the sensation of falling into a shaft with no bottom, of spinning helplessly into space. She tried to save herself but there was nothing to grab on to. The music stopped. Her hands lost their heat. The power that had helped her heal the white giraffe, a kudu and a leopard, drained from her heart. In its place was a desolate space, as icy as an underground cave.

A vivid light flashed. Someone was lifting her.

'I think the shock was too much for her,' her grandmother was saying as she dabbed at Martine's forehead with a damp cloth. 'I don't know what I was thinking, bringing her into the reserve at this hour. I should have known that the urge to help the rhino would have been too much for her to resist. I'll drive her home if you stay here with the vet. I think that's Johannes and the police approaching now.'

Martine opened her eyes. Tendai was cradling her in his broad black arms.

'You gave us quite a scare,' he said sternly. 'You fainted. I'm sorry for what you saw but you should not have followed us. It was for your own good that your grandmother told you to stay behind with Samson.'

'Put me down, Tendai,' said Martine, trying to wriggle free. 'I can help Cleo, you'll see.'

But even as she spoke, she knew it was wishful thinking.

Something had changed. Her gift had been taken from her; she'd felt it drain away.

'If you want to help, you'll allow your grandmother to take you home to bed,' said Tendai as he carried her to the Land Rover, shouldering his way through the long grass. Headlights showed through the trees. 'This is Johannes arriving now. If anyone can save Cleo, it's him. He's the best vet in the Cape.'

'But—'

'No buts,' said Gwyn Thomas, catching them up. 'We're going back to the house and we'll let the vet and the police do their job. I've got quite enough new grey hairs for one night.'

The stars were fading as Martine made her way up to bed. How she was expected to sleep with Spartacus dead, Cleo fighting for her life and their baby alone in the world she didn't know. Who could rest when the psychopaths who'd savaged them were on the loose?

But Gwyn Thomas had insisted. 'Don't worry, I'll be staying awake to speak to the police when they're finished in the game reserve. The focus of their investigation will doubtless be the Leopard Rock poachers, but they may have some questions about our guest list earlier in the evening.'

Martine was confused. 'What does that have to do with anything? I mean, we were with our guests the whole time. We watched them leave.'

She had a sudden memory of Lars and Kobe joking about robbing a bank so they could add rhino trophies to the bear and deer heads adorning the walls of their homes. Did they have connections in the underworld? Could Lars have done a deal in return for pinpointing the location of Sawubona's white rhinos?

Up in her room Martine messaged Ben. By the end of the Stars and Stripes evening, they'd barely been speaking. He'd made no secret of the fact that he was disappointed in her for being so starstruck, and she hadn't bothered to hide how annoyed she was with him for being such a killjoy. Take Flight had about ten million fans. It was hardly a crime if she was among them. Admittedly, she had a bit of a crush on Jayden, but that was because his music had a particular meaning for her. 'Song for Dad' had helped her through the toughest time of her life. It didn't mean that she had suddenly turned into a shallow, fame-obsessed loser.

Nonetheless, Ben was still her best friend. He was also clear-headed and dependable in a crisis.

She typed:

Poachers attacked our rhinos last nite. Worst thing ever. Wanna help me figure out how to catch the monsters who did it?

As she hit send, her gaze fell on the poster of Jayden, Liam and Lachlan that hung above the bookshelf. The guilty fear that she'd been shutting out since it had woken her at two a.m. returned with a vengeance.

She did an internet search on the elderly laptop given to her by her grandmother. She'd never used Twitter and didn't understand it, but Jayden's official account came up as soon as she punched in the first three letters of his name.

Her own face beamed back at her. There she was in the giraffe selfie with Jayden, smiling for the camera. It was hard to believe that barely eight hours had gone by since then. It felt like a lifetime.

She scrolled down Jayden's Twitter feed. There was a video clip from Take Flight's concert at Cape Town's Waterfront, loads of Tweets from devoted fans, and some banter between Jayden and Liam about Liam's new haircut.

Then it jumped out at her: a photo of Spartacus, Cleo and their baby attached to a Tweet.

saw this ace rhino family near troll bridge on the roybos river during stars 'n stripes safari at sawubona reserve nr cape town

The blood began to thrash in Martine's eardrums. 'No!' she said out loud. 'NO. This is not happening.'

Shoving the laptop away as if it were toxic, she hugged her knees. She was freezing cold.

'We have millions of fans on Twitter,' Jayden had told her, *'but I'm willing to bet that none of them are gun-toting wildlife criminals. Most of them are sweet kids like you.'*

What if he'd been wrong? What if one of those supposedly lovely fans or their family and friends was responsible for Spartacus's murder? What if by telling Jayden the name of the bridge and river, both well-known to local people, Martine had offered a GPS location to the poachers? Jayden had spelled Rooibos incorrectly, but that was unlikely to have deterred any potential killers. Somehow the poachers been able to fly directly to the clearing, dart the rhinos with tranquilisers and slice off their horns.

What if this whole awful tragedy was *her* fault?

The screensaver descended, obscuring Twitter. Numbly, Martine pressed a key. Jayden's newsfeed reappeared. Something was different; something that gave her heart palpitations. The rhino Tweet had gone viral.

· 8 ·

'I don't mind telling you I'm at my wit's end, Ben. It's been three days now. Three long days in which she's barely eaten and refused to go outside even to see Jemmy. He's been calling for her at the garden gate. You know how people are always saying that giraffes don't make a sound? It's not true. They make a musical fluttering noise. Except that now Jemmy sounds like a choirboy with laryngitis. He senses that there's something wrong with Martine and he's not the only one. I've called the doctor, but he's assured me she's not ill. According to him, it's all in her head.'

Gwyn Thomas's voice carried up the staircase. Through

the door it was distorted and distant, as if it was coming in on a crackling two-way radio and Martine's bed was a yacht in stormy seas.

'I blame myself,' she was telling Ben. 'I should never have taken Martine into the reserve on the night of the attack, but I was afraid to leave her in the house on her own when there was a chance that the poachers were still in the area. Now she's traumatised. Worst of all, she blames herself for not being able to heal Cleo. If only she'd see you, Ben. Maybe you could talk some sense into her. That's another mystery to me, why she doesn't want to talk to her closest friend. Have the two of you had a falling out?'

Ben made no response. Martine knew what he'd be thinking. He'd be confused and hurt that, having sent him a message asking him to come to Sawubona to help her figure out a way to track down the hunters who'd killed Spartacus and left Cleo for dead, she'd then told her grandmother to say she felt unwell and couldn't see him.

It wasn't a lie. She *was* sick – sick with guilt.

She was ill with tiredness too because the nightmares she'd suffered after her parents' death in the fire had returned with a vengeance. Over and over she'd relived the moment when she woke to find her room filled with smoke and flames crackling behind the door. In real life, she'd tied sheets together and escaped out of her second-storey window, but in the dream she found herself too scared to jump. She'd wake gasping for air and bathed in sweat, the bedclothes strangling her.

Martine had hoped that Ben would get fed up with

her excuses and go away, but he'd returned twice daily for three days in a row – every time he came to feed Shiloh. If he persisted, she'd have no choice but to see him. How could she play detective and go searching for clues, knowing all the while that she was hiding the biggest clue of all? How could she admit that she'd been so flattered by Jayden's attention that she'd given him the details that had guided the poachers to the rhinos? That she'd as good as signed their death warrant?

Martine wondered what would happen if she confessed everything to Ben. After all, he was the kindest, smartest boy she knew. If anyone was capable of understanding that she'd done a monumentally stupid thing and paid a terrible price for it, it was her best friend. But how could she expect him to forgive her when she could never ever forgive herself?

Until the poachers were caught, there was no way of knowing whether they'd read the Tweet or used some other method to find the rhinos, but Martine was convinced there could be no other explanation. It was hard to believe it was pure coincidence that the rhinos were attacked within a couple of hours of her conversation with Jayden. So far no one else knew about it, but she was gloomily sure that it was only a matter of time before she was dragged away in handcuffs.

The question going round and round in her head on an endless loop was who'd read the Tweet?

The problem was, there were thousands of possible suspects. The band had legions of South African fans. Any of them could have seen something on social media. Even before he left Sawubona, Jayden could have mentioned the rhinos' location near Troll Bridge on the Rooibos River to his manager or bandmates. They in turn could have spoken to a crew member, friend or record company person who just happened to have a part-time career as a poacher.

By that logic, Jayden, Liam and Lachlan were in the frame too, but Martine had already ruled them out. They were teenage millionaires, had the life of their dreams and were adored by millions. Why would any of them jeopardise that?

The same applied to their fat-cat manager. Martine had disliked Dirk on sight, but her grandmother had recently told her that all the latest science showed that it was nearly impossible to judge criminals by their appearance. Dirk was loud and a bit obnoxious, but he was also the highly successful manager of one of the biggest boy bands on the planet. The notion that he had a sideline in rhino poaching was laughable.

So who then? The police were focusing their efforts on finding the gang who'd attacked the Leopard Rock rhinos. They were sure the same men were responsible for both attacks. Martine was privately convinced that those particular poachers were long gone. Why would they hang around to be arrested? That meant that whoever had hacked off the horns of Spartacus and Cleo was still at large. Martine shivered at the thought.

Downstairs, Ben and Gwyn Thomas were discussing the rhino calf, now in Sawubona's wildlife hospital behind the house.

'I was sure that if anything could lift Martine's spirits it would be the adorable little rhino,' her grandmother was saying. 'Usually, it's impossible to keep her away from wild animals, especially the babies, but she doesn't want anything to do with him. I'm grateful to you for taking care of him, Ben. With Samson on sick leave, I don't know what we'd have done without you.'

Martine pulled the duvet over her head. That was another thing she felt guilty about – the baby rhino. She knew that he'd be lonely, scared and missing his mum, all things she'd felt when she arrived at Sawubona. But she couldn't face him. Not if it turned out that she was to blame for his suffering.

She couldn't face Jemmy either. Her healing gift had deserted her, leaving her afraid that she would no longer have a special bond with animals. She'd already lost her mum and dad. That was quite enough loss for one lifetime. If she ended up being rejected by both the white giraffe and Ben, she didn't think she could bear it.

If only she could turn back time. She'd rewind it to the morning of New Year's Eve, just over a year earlier, when her mum had produced surprise birthday cupcakes. The biggest one had eleven candles on it. Martine had blown them out in a single breath.

What had she wished for? She couldn't remember. Something trivial such as clothes or a phone. If she'd known what lay ahead, she'd have wished instead that someone would discover and fix the electrical fault that, hours later, would cause her home to burn to the ground.

But the clock had ticked relentlessly onward. It had

taken her loved ones with it and no scientist yet had come up with a way of manipulating time so that it returned parents and animals from the dead, or unsaid hurtful words, or undid idiotic mistakes.

Martine closed her eyes and burrowed deeper under the duvet. Her life was in ruins.

The sun peeped through a gap in the curtains and
tiptoed with fingers of light across the duvet,
which was powder blue and patterned with white
giraffes. Beneath it, Martine was dreaming – not
about the fire but about the rhinos. She was kneeling
beside Cleo, trying to comfort her. The mother rhino's
eye opened. This time her gaze was not accusing. It
was pleading. She spoke without words to Martine's
heart.

'Promise me you'll take care of my son, Jabulani.
Promise you'll find a safe place for Jabu.'

'I promise.'

It didn't feel weird to be giving her word to a rhino; somehow it felt right.

For the first time in days, Martine woke feeling peaceful. She stretched and slowly came to life. Then the guilt returned to crush her. Groaning, she pulled the covers over her head.

'Is that any way ta start tha day?' demanded a familiar voice, more Caribbean than African.

Martine shot up in bed. An extravagantly proportioned Zulu woman in vibrant traditional dress was burrowing through her chest of drawers. She counted out five T-shirts and added them to a half-packed suitcase.

'Grace, what on earth are you doing in my room? Why are you going through my stuff?'

The *sangoma* put a hand on one generous hip. 'Well, good mornin' to you too. I was goin' to say how great it is to see you, but now I'm not so sure.'

Martine reddened. 'I'm happy to see you too, Grace, but you'd also be freaked out if you woke up and found me rummaging through your belongings.'

'Freaked out? I don't think so. If you were packin' my suitcase, I'd assume that you and me, we were goin' travellin'.'

An unlikely vision of herself and Grace sitting side by side on a beach building sandcastles – perhaps in the Caribbean, the home of Grace's mother – came into Martine's mind. 'We're going on holiday together?'

'Not a holiday, hon. A journey. Very different thing.'

'My grandmother's put you up to this, hasn't she?' Martine said heatedly. 'Well, I've got news for you. I'm not going anywhere. I'm ill and it's not something that one of your potions can cure.'

'No? That's a real shame, 'cos I brought you a baobab smoothie. Not a problem. I can drink it myself.'

Martine wavered. Grace's smoothies were legendary. The baobab fruit one, which was made with powder from what the locals called the 'Tree of Life' was Martine's favourite. It also contained banana, almond milk, herbs, Chia seeds and local honey and was simply divine. 'Since you've gone to the trouble of making it, I'll try it, just in case it helps,' she suggested, snatching it off the bookshelf and taking a sip before Grace could change her mind.

The *sangoma* smiled. 'As you like.'

She tossed Martine's survival kit into the suitcase and sat down on the bed, causing it to sink and screech alarmingly. 'What's all this fuss about? What's got you tied up in knots?'

Martine swallowed the last of the smoothie and set the glass aside before answering. 'I can't tell you. You'd hate me. You'd never speak to me again. Then you'd tell Ben and my grandmother and they'd hate me too.'

'That so? You must be messed up in some bad business. What d'you do – steal a cookie?'

Martine glared at her. 'It's not funny. If you knew what I'd done, you'd know it's not something to joke about.'

Grace was silent for a moment. 'Chile, do you remember what I tole you the day we met, the same day you arrived in Africa?'

Martine did. It was engraved on her mind. Tendai had collected her from Cape Town airport and driven her into a world of dazzling colour and light, as far removed as Mars from the grey skies and snow she'd left behind in Hampshire, England. She'd been spellbound by Table Mountain and by the smoking waves, propelled up to the coast by a violent ocean of the fiercest blue.

En route to the house of the grandmother she'd never met, Tendai had made an unscheduled stop at the home of his aunt. Grace had laid a burning hot palm on her forehead and informed her that she had a gift. She'd not revealed what that gift was or how it would alter Martine's life. She'd only offered a warning.

'Be very careful. The gift can be a blessin' or a curse. Make your decisions wisely.'

'And have you?' Grace asked now. 'Have you made your decisions wisely?'

'No,' Martine confessed, 'I haven't. That's why I'm being punished. Grace, my gift has been taken away from me. It's gone. I was trying to heal Cleo, the mother rhino, and I felt the power drain out of me like a wave being sucked back into the sea.'

Grace took Martine's hand. 'One thing I can promise is that your gift will never leave you.'

'But it did! It has!'

'No, chile, *you* left your gift. There's a thorn in your heart that's blocking your healing energy. It ain't real, it's just in your mind.'

'But what can I do to fix things? Can you remove the thorn?'

'No one can do it for you, chile. It's your responsibility. You are the keeper of the key for your own heart. Your gift will be there when you need it but only if you *believe*.'

The air around Grace practically crackled with the force of her words. As always, Martine was part-soothed, part-terrified. But most of all she wanted to be close to the healer who had already taught her so much.

'Grace, is there any chance that you could read the bones and ask the spirits or the ancestors to tell you who attacked our rhinos?'

Grace pulled away. 'You should know better dan to ask me that. I ain't no fortune-teller.'

'Of course you are,' cried Martine. 'You're psychic. You've predicted things for me in the past and they've always come true. You helped me save Jemmy. Please, Grace. You could tell the police something that might lead to the capture of the poachers.'

The Zulu woman heaved herself to her feet, rainbow bracelets jingling. She made for the door, radiating disapproval.

Martine jumped out of bed. 'Grace, wait. I know you're not a fortune-teller. I'm sorry. It's been such a hideous few days and I've messed up so badly that I couldn't bear it if you turned away from me too. You said something about a journey. Where would you like to go to? I'll follow you to the ends of the earth if only you'll forgive me.'

Grace set down her bag. 'Oh, it won't be quite that far. If you follow me to Bloemfontein on tha nine o' clock train this morning, some good people are gonna collect you and take you to tha Golden Gate Highlands National Park.'

'*In San Francisco?*'

'No, the Golden Gate Highlands Park near Lesotho. It's just as beautiful but a whole lot more ancient.'

'If my grandmother is okay with it then, yes.'

'She's tha one who axed me to ax you about it. She wants you and Ben to accompany tha small rhino to her friends' sanctuary in tha Golden Gate National Park. I'm goin' to be visiting my grandchildren nearby so I tole her I'd take you most of tha way.'

'Ben's coming too? Then, no.'

'Fine,' shrugged Grace. 'No one's gonna force you to do nothin'. Up to you whether you stay here feelin' sorry for yourself or do a kindness for an innocent creature much worse off than you. Tha rhino baby, he's gettin' weaker every day. If he don't get the help he needs soon, he's gonna die for sure. You want that on your conscience?'

'No, but . . . '

A memory stirred in Martine's mind. *'Everything happens for a reason,'* her dad had told her just hours before the fire. Sometimes it was hard, if not impossible, to fathom what that reason could be, but since she'd arrived in Africa her dad's words had proved time and time again to be true. She couldn't change what had happened with Spartacus and Cleo, but she did have a chance to give their son a better future.

'Grace, what does *Jabulani* mean?'

'It's the Zulu word for rejoice. Why d'you want to know?'

Martine suddenly felt lighter. She'd made a promise and whatever it took she was going to honour it. 'Because that's the name of the rhino baby – Jabulani. Jabu for short.'

Grace accepted it without question. 'Good choice. Names are important. A beautiful name is gonna give him a beautiful future.'

Martine smiled for the first time since the night of the Stars and Stripes safari. She opened her cupboard. 'Okay, tell me what to pack.'

'My pleasure but in return I ask one small favour. Say goodbye to the white giraffe. Don't be afraid that some kind of magic between you has gone. Ain't nothing supernatural about the bond between you. You be friends for life. Tell Jemmy you have business to attend to and will be back soon enough. You need him as much as he needs you, but right now Jabu needs you most of all.'

· 10 ·

The train was grape-purple and powered by an orange locomotive. From a distance, it resembled an exotic caterpillar. Inside, the compartments were outfitted in matching purple velour and there was wood-panelling on the walls, plus a basin with soap, water and fluffy towels in one corner. Through the open window came the shouts of porters assisting boarding passengers, interspersed with platform announcements and a faraway Taylor Swift song. Martine hoped that Take Flight wasn't next on the playlist. She hadn't been able to listen to any of their music since the night of the rhino attack. Every note that Jayden sang would have been a reminder of what she'd done.

Hoisting her backpack higher on her shoulder, she turned to Ben. 'Which berth would you like?'

She felt shy and disconnected from him, as if the adventures they'd shared had never happened. It would have been easier if he'd shouted at her or been angry with her. That's what she felt she deserved. Instead they were both pretending that the past week had never happened. At the same time, there was something unspoken between them – an invisible barrier, covered by politeness.

'You choose,' said Ben.

'No, you choose.'

'Okay, I'll have the one on the right.'

'No, you won't,' interrupted Grace, powering in. 'Get your stuff. You're in the wrong compartment.'

'No we're not,' said Martine. 'Look, our names are on the door.'

Grace's only response was to whip their name tags out of the silver slot that held them and set off down the corridor. She barred the way of a man in a pristine navy blue suit, poised to wheel his case into number two.

'Sorry, sir, this compartment belongs to my young friends. Please step out of the way. If you are lost, number eleven is free.'

The man was indignant. 'I'm not lost. It says right here on my ticket—'

'Must be a misprint,' Grace said dismissively. 'Now are you goin' ta move along or d'ya want me to call security and tell 'em you're tryin' to steal the compartment of two chillun?'

He bristled. 'I'm not trying to steal anything. This is the

compartment I paid for and this is where I'll be staying.'

Grace leaned forward and whispered something in his ear. Whatever it was had an electrifying effect on him. Snatching up his suitcase, he strode away.

'All yours,' Grace announced, steering Martine and Ben into the compartment. 'Any 'mergencies, I'm in number five. See you at lunch.'

Martine tilted her shoulder and allowed her backpack to slide to the ground. 'What was that all about?'

Ben sank onto one of the purple berths and tested it for bounce. 'Don't know and I'm not sure I'm keen to find out. It's probably haunted or something.'

Martine suspected that the truth was not far off. She grinned. 'With Grace, anything is possible.'

Five words, but they went a long way to breaking the ice between them.

From the little Martine could recall of train journeys in England, the windows seldom opened. It scared her to think that those memories, as with so many from her childhood, were fading like photographs left out in the sun. It took effort to restore each one to full technicolour, but that's what she tried to do now, mentally exchanging the purple train for a rainy platform in Hampshire.

In winter, a man with mad professor hair used to roast chestnuts on a grill outside her local station. The memory of their charred sweetness was so vivid it made her mouth water. In the evenings, the tree-lined streets that led to her home had teemed with dog walkers and joggers. On frosty mornings the delicate skeletons of fallen oak leaves, their veins brushed with icicles, had made blue and brown patterns on the pavement.

'Don't go sticking your head out of the window or you might lose it,' cautioned Grace, putting her head round the door and interrupting Martine's thoughts. She was gone before either of the children could respond.

It was a good point. On African trains, windows opened wide because people liked to lean out and call to friends in passing villages, or spot wildlife. This was hazardous for any number of reasons, not least of which was passing trains.

For Martine and Ben, it was enough to have the breeze rushing in laden with sea-salt and the herby smell of heathery *fynbos*. The train had left Cape Town at nine a.m. The city went by in strips of sea, beach and green. Pastel cottages huddled in the folds of Table Mountain.

Then came the townships on the outskirts of town. Martine and Ben couldn't bear to see them. It made them furious that, in one of Africa's richest nations, thousands were crammed into shacks made of rotting wood and rusting corrugated iron, freezing in winter and sweltering in summer. The world of the townships was violent and desperate. People did what they needed to do to survive.

When human life had so little value, it was hardly surprising that rhinos were considered fair game.

The townships were an unwelcome reminder that the poachers were still on the loose. Martine was glad when the slums receded into the distance and they saw other, more hopeful sights. South Africa was like a world in one country. If you tired of creased purple mountains, Cape Dutch houses and vineyards, all you had to do was wait five minutes. Next time you looked there'd be ostriches pecking at the scorched ochre plains of the Karoo.

'I hope Jabulani isn't too frightened,' said Ben. 'He's had a nightmare week. He must be wondering what else life is going to throw at him.'

The thorn in Martine's heart dug deeper. So far she'd managed to avoid any contact with the baby rhino. It had been easier than expected because they'd left Sawubona less than twenty-four hours after Grace had told her about the plan to take the rhino calf to a sanctuary. Ben, Tendai and Johann the vet had loaded Jabu into his crate, ready for the journey. Martine had pretended to be extra busy helping her grandmother finalise travel arrangements and organise meals. She'd also said an emotional goodbye to Jemmy. It seemed he still loved her – even without her gift.

Now Jabulani was in a goods van, five carriages away, and Martine was running out of excuses not to see him.

'I have to feed him in a few hours so I guess I'll see how he is then,' said Ben. There was a question in his eyes. Martine flipped open her new book, *The Ghost Ship Mystery*. 'Good idea,' she mumbled without looking up.

At lunchtime they found Grace in a candy-striped booth in the dining car, looking strangely at home amid the polished silver cutlery and starched napkins. Her traditional dress was crimson and embroidered with yellow flowers. She'd accessorised it with a yellow scarf draped over one shoulder and a red headdress, drawing many admiring glances and some startled ones.

Just being with Grace made Martine feel better. It was impossible to be bored around her. She made them laugh with a story about an uncle who'd been chased by a lion while riding his bicycle. Exhausted and in despair, he'd flung down the bike and prepared to be eaten. But the lion was more interested in the bike. The last time the uncle saw the creature, it was gnawing happily on the leather seat.

The dining car emptied as they talked. Between apple pie and a mug of hot chocolate, Ben went to check on Jabulani. Left on her own with Grace, Martine felt exposed. The *sangoma* alone knew her secret. But Grace was preoccupied by the tea leaves at the bottom of her cup. She studied them with a disturbing intensity.

Finally, she handed the cup to a passing waiter and smiled warmly at Martine. 'This sanctuary where you're goin', who runs the place?'

'Glen and Susie Lowe. My grandmother has known them for decades. A couple of years ago, they started a rescue shelter for orphaned rhinos on the edge of the Golden Gate Highlands National Park. They don't keep any rhino older than two, so Jabu will be safe for the next couple of years at least. Poachers rarely waste their time with calves.'

Grace seemed distracted. She frowned at the passing

forests and drummed an aubergine-coloured fingernail on the table. There was no further conversation until Ben returned. Jabu was dopey from the sedative the vet had given him but, Ben said, doing well. He'd drunk a bottle of rhino milk before dozing off again. The guard had promised to keep a close watch on him.

Martine was only half-listening. She was convinced that the *sangoma* had glimpsed something in the tea leaves that she hadn't wanted to share. However much she tried to pretend otherwise, Grace had the gift of second sight.

'Grace, I'm worried about my grandmother and Jemmy,' she said. 'The police don't have a single lead on the poachers. What if they come back? My grandmother is alone in the house.'

But Grace wasn't thinking about Gwyn Thomas or Sawubona's wildlife. She was staring past Martine and Ben, into a dimension that was not of this world. It was a look they knew well and it almost always foreshadowed a coming storm. They glanced uneasily at one another.

'When I was a chile,' Grace began, 'my grandfather tole me many stories about the Gold Rush here in South Africa. It was in tha Witwatersrand region back in 1886. Ordinary men, decent men, family men, *sane* men became infected as if a worm had done burrowed into their brain. From one hour to tha next they were capable of anythin', even murder. Long as this sickness raged through their minds and bodies, they could not be trusted. Grandpa claimed that if you stared hard enough you could see the worm's eyes glowin' at the back of theirs.

Sometimes those eyes were green with envy. More times than not, they were blood-red with the lust for gold.'

Grace snapped out of her trance. Now when she looked at them, she was present. 'For poachers, rhino horn is the new gold. It causes tha same fever, tha same sickness. If you recognise it in any man, woman, boy or girl, don't try to be brave. Don't stand in their way. Just run.'

· 11 ·

Just run.

At one ten a.m., Grace's words were stuck on repeat in Martine's head. Not even the crisp white sheets or the *clickety-click* lullaby of the train on the tracks could soothe her. She was trying to recall the names of the guests at the Stars and Stripes safari. It was entirely possible that somebody there had been infected with the sickness Grace had spoken of; the lust for rhino gold. The blood-red eyes of the worm could have lurked behind theirs. Would she have spotted it if she'd seen it?

The Chans were the most obvious suspects. They were Hong King Chinese and China was the biggest market for rhino horn. Mr Chan had uttered few words during the course of the safari, but when he did speak he'd been sympathetic towards the customers who bought rhino products. He and his wife had left the dinner early because Mrs Chan supposedly had a migraine. Thomas, the new ranger, had driven them. Could he be in on it too? Could they have cooked up a plan together?

Thomas and the Chans were not the only possibilities. Mick had talked cheerfully about how a few rhino horns could be the passport to a stress-free life, where all he did was surf and chill out at the beach. Could he and an accomplice have seized the opportunity to make a killing?

The other thing keeping Martine awake was her promise to Cleo. She'd vowed to take care of Jabu, yet so far she'd avoided him. It had hurt too much to know that she might be part of the reason he was alone in the world now.

She glanced over at Ben. The rocking motion of the train sent starlight dancing like fairy dust across his face. He was probably dreaming about Shiloh. It had been a wrench for him to leave his new pony. It was a measure of how badly he'd wanted to help Jabu that he'd been prepared to give up a week of riding time to take the rhino calf to the Golden Gate Highlands.

This thought spurred Martine from her berth. Pulling her jeans on over her shortie pyjamas and grabbing her jumper and boots, she slipped into the corridor. The lights had been dimmed and gritty night air blasted in from an open window. Martine was tempted to go straight back to her bunk. She laced up her boots instead. Determinedly, she set off in the direction of the goods van.

The scariest part was crossing between carriages. The floor swayed horribly and she was convinced that they'd break apart at the exact moment she stepped from one to the next. She imagined herself doing the splits as they rattled away in opposite directions. Gaps in the floorboards revealed the tracks flashing below.

At one point she heard two loud thuds and a yell. She stopped, but there was no further sound. The temptation to fly back to the safety of her berth was strong, but her promise to Cleo drove her on.

As she walked, the carriages gave up clues about their occupants. A chainsaw snore. The growl of a small terrier. A couple arguing ('You said!' 'No, *you* said!').

Martine reached the goods van without seeing anything more sinister than a waiter reaching into a compartment for a tray. By contrast, the goods van was crammed with crates, mailbags and trunks, which creaked and groaned like a haunted house. Black shadows boxed on the walls. The guard was not on guard. Martine suspected he was taking a sneaky nap.

Her hope was that the rhino's crate would be obvious, but it wasn't. She had to scramble over the piles of mailbags and lift the tarpaulins on various crates. One contained two small but energetic crocodiles. Martine almost dropped dead from fright. She wished she'd come earlier with Ben. That way, she'd know exactly where to find Jabu.

A sad squeak finally led her to the furthest corner of

the goods van. The rhino was lying in an untidy heap on the floor of his crate. He looked like a lily-eared alien. Martine did her best to calm him through the wire mesh, but it had no effect. He was panting with fear. She was afraid he might die.

On the spur of the moment, she opened the crate door and climbed in. Jabu squeaked with alarm. Martine expected the guard to come running, but the goods van stayed dark. When she touched the little rhino, he trembled so much that it brought tears to her eyes. Once she'd had the power to make even a savage leopard trust her. Now with her gift gone, Jabulani saw her as just another human with the potential to cause him pain.

'I gave your mum my word that I would look after you,' she whispered to him. 'Somehow I have to find a way to do that. I know you're frightened and lonely, but so am I. Maybe we can find a way to help each other.'

She curled up against his grey belly and rested her cheek again his ribcage. He squeaked again and his heart pounded madly in her ear. Martine did the only thing she could think of to soothe him. She recited a William Blake poem she'd had to learn for an exam.

Tyger! Tyger! Burning bright, In the forests of the night; What immortal hand or eye. Could frame thy fearful symmetry?

In terms of content, it wasn't the best choice, but it did the trick. Jabu's pulse and breathing slowed. So did Martine's. As she melted into sleep, their hearts were beating in sync.

Ben came to find her at three a.m. to tell her that their train would shortly be arriving in Bloemfontein, where they were getting off. He would have come earlier but he'd bumped into the guard, who was in a state of high excitement. There'd been an attempted robbery on compartment eleven. It turned out that a thief had been plaguing the train. The rail company had hushed it up for fear of bad publicity. They'd suspected a regular passenger adept at disguise. Until tonight, they'd failed to catch him or her.

The last thing Ben would have wanted was for himself and Martine to fall victim to a robber. However, it worried him that by switching their compartment Grace had seen to it that some other innocent person suffered that fate.

She knew, he thought. *The canny old* sangoma *knew all along that compartment eleven would shortly be a crime scene.*

'It was a lucky day for us that the thief chose number eleven,' the guard told him. 'The passenger he tried to rob was a Seventh Dan in Taekwondo. Two blows and the man was subdued. I have locked the thief in another compartment and he will be arrested as soon as we reach Johannesburg. The police are meeting the train.'

When Ben finally reached the goods van and opened the baby rhino's crate, there was such a tangle of limbs he couldn't tell where Jabu ended and his best friend began.

For the first time since the fateful night of the Stars and Stripes safari, he allowed himself to feel hopeful. Everything would be all right in the end.

Probably.

'Welcome to the Golden Gate Sanctuary, kids. You must be starving after the long drive. Personally, I could eat a grilled rhino with some apricot chutney on the side. Ah, here comes my wife, Susie. She'll show you to your quarters. By the time you've showered, our famous Golden Gate breakfast will be ready. Is it poached peacock today, darling, or is Chef serving *my* favourite, zebra fritters?'

Martine, who was clambering stiffly out of the SUV, froze in mid-exit. She and Ben exchanged appalled glances. Glen Lowe, a man with a girth like a baobab and a beard like a hedge that needed trimming, didn't notice. He had their rucksacks in one huge paw and was hugging Susie with the other. Laughing, his wife wriggled free. She slapped him lightly on the arm. A pocket-sized redhead, she embraced the children as if they were long-lost friends.

'Don't mind Glen's sense of humour. He's the biggest softie on earth when it comes to rhinos – especially the babies. There hasn't been a rhino calf born that isn't capable of turning him into a marshmallow with one bat of its eyelashes. He's also a vegetarian like you so you needn't worry that we'll be feeding you Springbok burgers. Now I suggest that you leave Jabulani in Glen's capable hands and I'll show you to your rooms. How was your journey? Was it gruelling?'

After a fifteen-hour train ride, followed by a three-and-a-half-hour drive, Martine was in a fog of exhaustion. Leaving Ben to answer Susie's questions, she sucked in a big breath of dust perfumed with honeysuckle and rhino. *This is how Africa climbs into your heart,* she thought. *It invades your nostrils; flies into your ears on the songs of robins, turtle-doves and Go-Away birds; fills your vision with heavenly vistas.* The one beyond the boundary fence was a timeless African scene of washed-out blue hills, thatched huts and waving grassland dotted with zebras. Distant sandstone cliffs glowed gold in the morning sun.

'Now you know how the area gets its name,' said Susie, as she led them through a garden twitching and shimmering with butterflies and birds. Neatly painted wooden signs directed visitors to the Main Reception, the Calabash Café, the Rhino Nursery and the Main House.

Ten thatched cottages with chocolate brown walls were scattered among the trees. Theirs was number seven. It had an open-plan kitchen and living room decorated with a fat brown leather sofa, colourful Basotho rugs and an oil painting of a lion. On the kitchen table was a vase filled with orange and yellow wildflowers.

There were three bedrooms upstairs. The biggest was being used by Amelia, a German volunteer.

'I thought it might be fun for you to hang out with someone closer to your own age in the evenings rather than being stuck up at the main house with us old fogies,' Susie said with a smile. 'During the day you'll be so busy with the rhino babies that you won't have time to be lonely. You'll take your meals with the other volunteers in the Calabash Café. If there's an emergency or if you simply have a question, use your cottage phone to dial 121. That's the main house. Glen or I will help you with anything you need.

'By the way, we have a strict no-phone policy around the rhino. Our orphans have been through quite enough already without being subjected to endless beeps, trills and Tweets. I'd be grateful if you'd give me yours for safe-keeping. Any time you want to call home, feel free to use the landline.'

She handed them a couple of black T-shirts with the Golden Gate sanctuary logo on the front. 'A gift to help you feel at home with us. From what I've heard, you've both been through hell. I'm hoping that, along with helping Jabulani settle in, you'll enjoy seeing some of the park's famous attractions. I understand that your friend

Grace will be escorting you back to Cape Town in five days' time, ready for high school. Looking forward to it?'

'Sort of,' said Ben.

'Not really,' admitted Martine.

Susie laughed. 'That's how I felt, but it turned out to be one of the best experiences of my life. Besides, you've come to the perfect pre-high school training ground. If you can cope with young rhino, you'll find teenagers a breeze.'

Breakfast in the Calabash Café was hash browns, herby tomatoes, fried banana and huge eggs the colour of sunshine.

'Dinosaur eggs,' Glen informed them gravely. 'What – you don't believe me?'

He pointed his fork at a poster explaining that the oldest dinosaur embryos ever discovered were found in the Golden Gate Highlands National Park in 1978. The eggs contained the fossilised foetal skeletons of the Massospondylus, a herbivorous dinosaur from the Triassic Period.

'That's 220–195 million years ago, so you see, your eggs have had plenty of time to mature and develop complex flavours. You have signed a disclaimer, haven't you? If your canine teeth grow or you turn into a Thecodontia dinosaur – they're these cool crocodile dinosaurs – we can't be held responsible.'

'Mr Lowe winding you up about the food again?'

demanded the chef, coming over with two mugs of malted chocolate milk. 'Don't worry, you'll get used to it. We have. Every now and then we get our revenge by slipping a minced-up Christmas beetle into his soup, but—'

Glen went a puce colour. 'Carlos, you wouldn't ... would you? I'm a vegetarian!'

The chef grinned. 'All I'm saying is, everyone has limits.'

'Okay, okay. Point taken.'

Carlos nudged Martine. 'Just so you know, I collected these eggs myself not thirty minutes ago. They were still warm from the nest when I put them in the pan.'

Suitably reassured, the children dived into breakfast. As they munched, they saw Glen's serious side, the side that had made him South Africa's leading expert on orphaned rhinos.

'You've done the right thing, bringing Jabulani to us when you did. One day longer and you might have lost him. We've put him on a drip ... '

Martine paled. 'Is he going to die?'

'I doubt it. When your grandmother described how listless he was and said that she and Ben were struggling to get him to eat, I have to admit I was worried. But it's almost as if that Jabu has been swapped with another on the train. The new Jabu is dehydrated and still grieving for his mum, but seldom have I seen an orphan with more fighting spirit. He wants to live. When that happens, the battle is almost won.'

Which battle? thought Martine. *What happens when he's older and a poacher wants his horn?*

Then the real meaning of Glen's words filtered through. On the train, Jabu had somehow regained his fighting spirit. Her heart gave a little skip. Maybe, just maybe, she'd helped by bonding with him.

Ben was thinking exactly the same thing.

Glen wiped his beard with his napkin and pushed back his chair. 'Now if you're done with the dinosaur eggs, I'll give you a guided tour and introduce you to some of our team. I can't wait for you to meet the stars of our Rhino Nursery.'

· 13 ·

The first surprise was that Jabulani would be sharing a pen with a white-and-chestnut goat with a wicked set of horns.

'I know what you're thinking,' said Glen. 'You're wondering if we've lost our minds putting Jabu into an enclosure with Billy rather than into the nursery with the other orphans. Am I right?'

Amelia, who had a honey-coloured ponytail and a tan to match, winked at Martine and Ben. 'I dare you to tell him he's crazy.'

What nobody could deny was that Jabu, though wobbly, seemed reborn. Transfixed by his odd companion, he'd barely glanced up as the children came through the gate. The goat cared only about breakfast. Munching peacefully, he stared off into space as if hanging around rhinos was an everyday event for him.

Jabu shuffled nearer. He attempted a playful pirouette. Even that didn't get the goat's attention. Stretching out his nose, he nibbled Billy's ear to test if it was edible. The goat gave a warning toss of his horns but carried on eating. Losing patience, the rhino shoved his nose under Billy's belly and lifted him off his hooves.

'Aren't you going to stop this before one of them gets hurt?' demanded Martine as the goat bleated frantically.

Glen grinned. 'If I had a dollar for every time someone said that to me, I'd be driving a Ferrari. You have my word that I'll step in if I'm the least bit concerned.'

In the next instant, the goat took a running jump and landed on Jabu's back. For a moment, the rhino was too stunned to react. Then he took off like a bronco at a Wild West Show.

Martine and Ben burst out laughing. It was the funniest thing they'd ever seen and, they quickly realized, one of the most joyful. Before their eyes, an unlikely friendship was blossoming.

Each time Billy was catapulted off Jabu's back, the calf would nuzzle him until the goat was once again persuaded to use him as a rhino trampoline. In between, they played chase. Just as Martine was starting to fret that Jabu might be overdoing things, he slowed like a toy with a dying battery. His legs crumpled beneath him. He was asleep almost before his eyes closed. Billy snuggled up against his belly. Resting his head on the rhino's chest, he too dozed off.

Martine was enraptured. 'That's too adorable.'

As she spoke, she heard a giggle. Through a slit in the wooden fence, she spied dusty brown skin and eyes as dark and sparkling as those of Echo the bush baby. She smiled and took a step closer.

Instantly the face was withdrawn. The soft slap of bare feet running faded into the distance.

As Glen closed the gate on the sleeping animals, Martine squinted into the sunlight. At the rear of the sanctuary a sandy track cut through the trees to a village of thatched huts. She wondered if it was to there that the girl had run.

Ben was plying Glen with questions. 'What made you think that those two species would get along so well? How did you know they wouldn't attack each other? What made you think they could be friends?'

Glen was amused. 'Ben, I wish I could claim credit for being an animal behaviour wizard, but there's nothing fantastical involved. Billy has been with us for a couple of years. We rescued him as a kid from an abusive owner. He was minutes away from the cooking pot, although I doubt he'd have been good for anything but soup. You could count every rib on him. As he grew and became stronger, we discovered something interesting. He was drawn to orphaned rhino, especially those who were as sick or as unhappy as he'd once been. Just as importantly, they adored him. Now he's our chief foster parent for all new babies.

'The difference between humans and animals is that

animals don't see difference as a negative thing. All they care about is kindness. If they find a friend, they don't care if that friend is a zebra, a one-eyed parrot or a tortoise. Even species that are traditionally mortal enemies, like leopards and impala, will make an exception if a particular set of circumstances creates a friendship between them.'

He took a bunch of keys from his pocket and unfastened a complicated system of chains and locks.

'In case you're wondering, we don't have these to keep any criminals out,' Amelia said with a smile, 'we have them to keep the rhino in. They're the Houdinis of the animal world.'

'But how?' asked Martine. 'What do they use – their teeth?'

'Their horn. Don't be fooled into thinking they're clumsy. When it comes to picking locks, they'd put a safe-cracker to shame.'

The gate swung open on the Rhino Nursery. The cuteness factor was off the charts. Nine orphans were in varying states of bliss. Two were napping in the shade, four were jostling for control of a big pink Swiss ball and the remaining babies were playing in a muddy wallow. They were coated from head to toe in glistening red clay. To Martine, it looked as if they were smiling.

'Who knew that rhinos were this much fun?' said Ben, watching the baby rhinos pursuing their pink ball like stumpy footballers.

Amelia tutt-tutted teasingly. 'You hadn't heard that next to the word "fun" in the dictionary, there's a picture of a baby rhino? Seriously, these little guys will play all day long if you let them. When they're not napping, that is. They do enjoy their sleep. Like me! My friends say that if a brass band played a concert in my bedroom, I wouldn't stir.'

A Xhosa man in a khaki ranger's outfit was adding water to the mud in the wallow. He greeted them with a leathery handshake.

'Meet Goodwin,' said Glen. 'He's our nursery manager. We'd be lost without him and his nephew . . . Ah, here's Victor now.'

Victor wore small round glasses with spindly frames that kept sliding down his nose like an out-of-control skier. His crisp white shirt and tweed waistcoat was an odd choice for a job involving close contact with wild animals, but Martine thought it suited him. Apart from his glasses, he looked smart and professional.

'Victor is a second-year veterinary student who volunteers at Golden Gate whenever he gets a break,' said Glen. 'He's a bright young man and we're lucky to have him.'

His phone buzzed. He glanced at it with a frown and stepped away to reply to a message.

'Victor is the first boy in our village to go to university,' beamed Goodwin.

His nephew pushed up his glasses and held them fast to the bridge of his nose.

'That's fantastic, Victor,' said Martine. 'You must be so proud. It's my dream to be a vet when I grow up.'

'It's a great job, but there's a lot of sacrifice and study. Don't go to veterinary school if you want to get rich quick.'

Martine was taken aback. 'I don't care about the money. All I want to do is help animals.'

'My nephew is joking,' Goodwin assured her. 'Victor, what's up with you? Did you get out of bed on the wrong side this morning?'

'I think becoming a vet is a wonderful goal,' said Amelia, smiling encouragingly at Martine. 'You've got off to a great start by rescuing Jabu. Thank you for coming all the way from Cape Town to bring him to our sanctuary. We're sad when a new orphan comes to us because we know what it means, but at the same time we rejoice because each baby rescued is a rhino saved.'

'What happens when your orphans grow up?' asked Ben. 'Are you ever tempted to keep them?'

'Never,' said Glen, striding over 'They belong in the wild and that's where we return them.'

'But—'

Glen's phone buzzed again. 'Sorry, kids, I have urgent business to attend to. I'll leave you in the capable hands of Goodwin and Amelia. They'll assign you a few chores. I hope Gwyn warned you that Golden Gate is not a holiday camp. We're permanently short-staffed and don't have that luxury.'

The German girl watched him go, a small crease between her eyes. 'Poor Glen. This is the best job in the world but it comes at a price.'

Martine remembered thinking the same thing about Tiffany, Take Flight's stiletto-wearing PR. 'And what price is that?'

It was Victor who answered. 'Blood, sweat and tears.'

Bronze bars of sunset were slanting through the trees as Martine skipped up the path to Rhino HQ, a two-room, corrugated-iron-roofed building that served as office, storeroom and rhino treatment centre. Her muscles ached. Earlier, she and Ben had been assigned their tasks. The sanctuary had six Basotho ponies, most of which were used to take visitors on horseback safaris, and Ben had been ecstatic to learn that he'd be working as a groom at the stables.

'None of the ponies is as pretty as Shiloh,' he confided to Martine, 'but from what I can tell they have all the characteristics that make Basothos special. They're tough, gentle and loyal. If I gain more experience, it'll be good for Shiloh.'

Martine's role was to help out with Jabu and at the nursery, and to fetch and clean bottles for the calves at feeding times. That's where she was going now.

It was shortly after six p.m. and Rhino HQ was deserted. Susie, who did the sanctuary accounts, had returned to the house she shared with Glen. Martine let herself in and put her pouch on the silver examining bench. On the wall opposite was a whiteboard chart with the formula for each rhino's bottle. Jabu's feed contained cooked rice, a dash of apple juice, clover, colostrum and skimmed milk packed with vitamins. Victor, who was supposed to be mixing it, was nowhere to be seen.

She was about to leave when she heard the tapping of computer keys. Victor was bending over a toy helicopter in the office. On the laptop screen behind him was a fuzzy grey satellite image of a landscape with black dots on it.

Some sixth sense told him he was being watched. His shoulders stiffened. Clutching the helicopter to his chest, he spun round in his chair.

'I've come to get the milk for the orphans,' Martine said quickly.

He glowered at her for a moment before deciding she hadn't intended to spy on him. 'Sorry, I lost track of time . . . I've been trying to fix something.'

Martine took a couple of steps nearer. 'Is that a remote control helicopter?'

He held it up, his glasses glinting in the light. 'Actually it's a drone. There's a camera inside. It's part of a project I've been working on at veterinary school. We're developing drones that can patrol game reserves at night, using infrared technology to spot poachers. The idea is that fewer rangers can cover much greater distances, as well as being able to see in the dark. If they spot poachers moving in on a rhino or elephant, they can dispatch an anti-poaching unit to deal with them before it's too late. As it stands now, many rangers find themselves scrambling to respond sometimes hours after the event.'

'I wish we'd had a drone at Sawubona when poachers attacked our rhinos,' sighed Martine. 'Maybe we could have saved Spartacus and Cleo.'

She pictured hundreds of drones whizzing across Africa, alerting the authorities to the evil activities of poachers everywhere. Perhaps she could ask for a drone of her own for her birthday. That way, she could keep an eye on Jemmy.

Victor was examining the underside of the helicopter, where the camera was stored. He gave a click of annoyance. 'Technology. Why is it always going wrong?'

Slamming his laptop shut, he stood up and gave her a broad smile. 'Right, let's get these rhino fed.'

Ten pink bottles were mixed and ready to go when Martine noticed that the embroidered pouch in which she kept her survival kit, was missing.

'Sure you didn't leave it at the nursery?' asked Victor.

He checked his watch, eager to get back to repairing his drone.

Martine was positive. Her pouch was her most precious possession. She never went anywhere without it. In it were six small blue bottles of healing herbs given to her by Grace. There was also a Swiss Army knife with a variety of useful attachments, a Maglite torch, a crepe bandage and some gauze, plus a book. Martine loved reading and never went anywhere without a mystery novel or one about animals. The thought that someone might have run off with these special things made her frantic.

'Call the police. I have to find my pouch, I absolutely have to.'

Victor smiled ruefully. 'I hate to break it to you but the police are not going to waste their time hunting for a child's purse – not unless it contains diamonds and rubies. Does it?'

His tone was gently teasing but Martine gave him a cold stare. 'The contents of my pouch are worth more to me than all the diamonds in Africa. Besides, I haven't finished reading my detective story and I was just getting to the good part.'

His expression changed. 'Are you saying there was a book in your bag?'

'Uh, yes.'

'In that case, I'm pretty sure I can lay my hands on the thief.'

He marched into the yard, reached up into a mango tree and grabbed a bare brown foot. A scrap of a girl came tumbling out, spitting and hissing like a feral kitten. Her face was almost completely obscured by dreadlocks. *The Ghost Ship Mystery* smacked onto the grass beside her. Martine was startled to recognise the urchin she'd glimpsed through the fence that morning.

The girl tried to dart away, but Victor grabbed her arm. 'You're right, Martine, let's call the police. They can lock up this no-good thieving brat and throw away the key. She's been banned from the sanctuary for stealing, but Security seem to find it impossible to keep her out.'

Martine was shocked. 'Victor, leave her alone. You're hurting her. You can't call the police. She's just a kid.'

'No, I'm not, I'm almost twelve.' The girl wore a too-big dress that might once have been yellow. She was small for her age, but her clear, confident voice was that of someone taller, older, wiser and a lot less grubby. 'And I wasn't stealing your book, I was *borrowing* it. There's a difference.'

'When you borrow something, it's polite to ask first,' Martine said firmly but not unkindly.

'You're wasting your time trying to teach her manners,' said Victor, securing his glasses to the bridge of his nose with one hand and gripping the girl's arm with the other. 'She doesn't know the meaning of the word "Please". She's stolen my university books and returned them weeks later dog-eared and covered in mulberry juice stains. Anyone would think that she was the one studying for a degree.'

'At least I *read* them and don't waste my time playing cards on a computer like you,' jeered the girl.

'Don't believe a word of it, Martine. If she was that

keen on reading, she'd go to school. Glen and Susie pay her tuition fees, but she's barely spent a day in class all term. She's the worst truant they have.'

'That's because they study babyish subjects I'd forgotten about by the time I was seven,' the girl informed him. 'I asked the teacher a question about DNA and she looked at me as if I was speaking Latin. In case you missed that day at vet school, Victor, DNA's short for Deoxyribonucleic acid – the genetic code for all living things. Yours is probably quite simple.'

She evaded him easily as he lunged at her. Martine stepped between them.

'Look, I don't care what you have or haven't done. All I want is my pouch. It was the last thing my mum gave to me before she died so it means a lot. The book you can have with pleasure.'

'I thought you said you'd just got to the exciting part, Martine,' accused Victor.

'I had, but I'm sure they'll have a copy in the library of my new school. I can finish it there. Or maybe . . . ' She turned to the girl. 'What's your name?'

'Sfiso. It means wish. Some people call me Saf.'

A strange feeling came over Martine. It was the same one she'd experienced when she curled up in the crate with Jabu – as if someone was shining a light into her guilty heart. She smiled. 'When you've finished the book, Saf, maybe you can tell me how it ends? If you want to, that is. It doesn't matter if you don't.'

Victor was incredulous. 'You're rewarding her for stealing your stuff?'

'She didn't *steal* my book. She borrowed it. Now I'm giving her permission to keep it. She borrowed my pouch too and any minute now she's going to return it.' Martine said this last part hopefully.

The girl shimmied up the tree and retrieved the pouch from a hollow high in the trunk. When she came down, there were wet streaks in the dust on her face. 'I didn't break anything, I swear. I was only curious. If I'd known it was given to you by your mum, who you lost, I'd never have borrowed it.'

Across the fields came the jangling of cowbells and the songs of the evening birds. In the nursery, the rhino babies were squeaking for their dinner.

Martine traded the *Ghost Ship Mystery* for her pouch. 'Forget it. I have. Hope you enjoy this. It had me hooked.'

Sfiso didn't smile back. She snatched the book and held it tightly in case Martine changed her mind.

'Now get lost,' said Victor. 'If I catch you within a hundred metres of Rhino HQ at any time in the next decade, I will be calling the police – don't think I won't.'

The girl was gone in a second, a shadow among shadows.

Amelia came hurrying up the path. 'What's the hold-up? If the rhino have to wait any longer for their bottles, we'll get trampled in the crush.'

'It's my fault,' said Martine. 'I thought I'd lost my pouch. Victor helped me find it. The bottles are ready. Give me a minute to grab them and I'll deliver them to the nursery faster than a flying cheetah.'

At one a.m. Ben gave up on sleep and went down to the living room. He fixed himself a mug of chocolate milk and sat on the sofa with the mini iPad his dad had brought him when he last sailed to Dubai. The same thought that had kept him awake for days was keeping him awake now: Martine had a painful secret. He wished that she'd trust him enough to confide in him. It didn't take a brain surgeon to guess that it had something to do with the rhino attack at Sawubona. What was more difficult to fathom was why she blamed herself.

He typed in his password and clicked on a folder. Up came the guest list for the Stars and Stripes safari.

Topping it were the Take Flight boys, their manager Dirk and their PR girl, Tiffany.

Ben had an almost physical reaction to the words on the screen. From the moment Jayden Lucas had stepped off the helicopter, Martine had been different. Ben had known for a while that she loved the band's music, but he'd never seen Martine in fan-girl mode before. It had made him uncomfortable and . . . well, jealous.

It wasn't that he imagined that she'd suddenly become Jayden or Liam's best friend. Pop idols didn't work that way and neither did Martine. She loved nature and sleeping under the stars and the simple things in life. The fake, glittery world of celebrity would soon bore her.

The real reason Ben had been upset to see Martine taking Jayden and Olivia to meet Jemmy was that it had given him a taste of what to expect at high school. Ben was deeply shy and found it easier to talk to horses and dogs than people. Before Martine had walked into his life, he'd been the loneliest boy in Storm Crossing, forever being bullied and mocked. Martine had changed that. He'd helped her rescue the white giraffe from hunters and she in turn had invited him into her world.

It was a world where there were as many dangers as there were miracles, but not for anything would he turn back the clock. During their adventures, he'd reached inside himself and found reserves of strength and courage he never knew existed. He'd survived on an island, swum with dolphins, touched leopards, walked with elephants and learned to track and to ride.

The new school threatened all of that. In weeks to

come, Martine would meet dozens of new friends and that would be good for her, but it might also mean that she realised that he, Ben, was quite dull by comparison.

'Penny for your thoughts?'

Ben jumped. Recovering, he said lightly: 'You're not in Hampshire now. We use Rand in South Africa. Trust me, my thoughts aren't worth even one of those.'

Martine sank into the brown leather sofa beside him. She noticed the guest list on his screen. 'Looking for suspects?'

'I was thinking about it. Any ideas?'

'You can cross the Take Flight boys off the list for starters. They're teenage millionaires living the dream. To suspect them of flying round Africa chopping off rhino horns is just stupid.'

Ben was stung. 'Maybe it is, maybe it isn't. I mean, they have plenty of money to pay someone else to do it for them.'

Their gazes locked in a battle so fierce that Ben could almost hear the scrape of swords. Martine's shoulders slumped. 'You're right. We can't cross anyone off the list. We need to find as much background information as we can about every guest at the dinner. Guilty until proven innocent, that should be our motto.'

Ben hid his relief. 'We could call our investigation Operation Rhino in honour of Ian Player. I saw a documentary about him recently. He was this legendary Zululand game warden who saved the Southern White Rhino from extinction in the sixties by sending them to zoos and safari parks all over the world. Like you, I believe every rhino should have the right to be free, but so many were being killed that Dr Player decided it was the only way to conserve the species. And he was right. The Southern White Rhino survived and the Northern White Rhino didn't. There's only one male left in the world. His name's Sudan and he's guarded twenty-four hours a day in Kenya. When he dies, his species will be extinct apart from four females in zoos around the world.'

'All the more reason why we need to track down the poachers who attacked Sawubona's rhinos before they strike again,' said Martine. 'When my grandmother called earlier, she said the police are getting nowhere fast. It's up to us to solve the mystery. Operation Rhino's a perfect code name. How about dividing the guest list in half? You investigate the first twelve names and I'll do detective work on the rest.'

Ben read between the lines of what she was saying. If a member of Take Flight was somehow linked to the crime, she didn't want to be the first to find out. 'Sure?'

'Absolutely certain. Now Amelia told us that a brass band playing on her bed wouldn't wake her, but there's no point in taking chances. Don't waste time reading things tonight, just download them. I'll use the house PC. It's ancient but Amelia says it works. Anything I find, I'll email to you. We can cross-check everything later.'

They worked as quickly as they could, but by two-fifteen a.m., both were yawning.

'We should sleep,' said Ben.

'We should,' agreed Martine, 'but maybe we should check on Jabu before we turn in.'

Walking through the moonlit garden, they swapped stories of their experiences that day. Martine told Ben about her encounter with Sfiso.

'She's this scraggly, bony girl who's our age and looks about nine, but she's super-smart. Victor doesn't like her. In a way you can't blame him because she takes his university books without asking, but I think he's secretly scared that she's cleverer than him. Amelia does some fundraising for the local school and she told me that Saf lives with a teenage aunt. Her mum ran off with some jazz musician years ago and she was brought up by her dad. He was a paleontologist – a fossil scientist – who used to work in the Golden Gate Highlands National Park.'

'Used to?'

'He died of pneumonia nine months ago. Amelia says that ever since then Saf's run wild. Nobody can control her – not the police, social workers, teachers or her aunt. Glen and Susie knew her father well and they've tried to help, but she causes trouble everywhere she goes. She and her dad were very close. He home-schooled her, though Amelia told me that mostly consisted of her assisting him on digs and excavations in the National Park. They went everywhere together.'

'Poor girl' said Ben. 'I'm glad you gave her your book. I'll give her mine if I see her. It's a survival story set in the Antarctic. It's brilliant.'

As his torch lit the path to the nursery the orphans snuffled nervously. A pinprick of yellow light gleamed through the trees. Martine wondered if Victor was still tinkering with his drone. She'd always assumed that people who studied veterinary medicine wanted a hands-on job healing animals, but perhaps that wasn't true. There were other ways of making a difference. Victor's poacher-spotting drone was one of them.

Jabu and Billy were snuggled together in the corner of their enclosure. When Ben unlocked the gate, they lurched forward on unsteady legs, blinking sleepily. Martine leaned down and breathed into the rhino's nose. He breathed back at her – two short puffs and three long, like rhino Morse code.

'Ben, listen to this,' she said excitedly. 'Glen told me that the vocabulary of rhinos is larger and easier to understand than almost any mammal apart from primates and dolphins. They breathe in patterns. All you have to do is work out what the patterns mean and you can understand what they're trying to tell you.'

Ben grinned. 'Wouldn't that be cool? What do you think they'd say at our new school if we told them we could speak Rhino.'

'They'd say we were nuts,' Martine said wryly. 'Which we are. Why else would we be playing with a rhino and a goat at this time of the morning?'

Ben jumped up. 'Where's the goat? Martine, where's Billy?'

The gate was open.

Pausing only to latch it so the rhino didn't escape as

well, they flew into the garden. Billy was in the vegetable patch behind the kitchen. Cheeks stuffed with carrots, he reluctantly allowed himself to be led back to his enclosure.

In the meantime, Jabulani had undone the latch. He was exploring too. It turned out that baby rhinos are a whole lot harder than goats to round up, not least because they weigh as much as three grown men. Despite this, Jabu was as agile as a hare. He led them on several exhausting circuits of the garden, leaping flowerbeds and ditches, before they coaxed him into his enclosure with two sugar cubes Ben found in his pocket.

'Now I know how horses feel after they've competed in the Grand National,' said Martine, tiredly attempting to brush mud and burrs off her jeans.

Jabu looked very pleased himself. He breathed at her through the bars of the gate.

'I can guess what that meant,' remarked Ben. 'He's saying, "That was a blast. Any time you want to play that game again, I'll be ready and waiting."'

Martine blew into the rhino's nostrils. 'Know what that means, Jabu? It's human for "Thanks, but no thanks. Maybe next century. Susie's going to murder us when she finds what you've done to her hydrangeas."'

'She will,' agreed Ben. 'And if we're still alive when Carlos sees the wreckage of his vegetable patch, we'll be eating stale bread and water for the rest of—'

He clutched Martine's arm. 'Look – through the trees! Glen's coming. Goodwin's with him.'

She panicked. 'We can't let Glen catch us here. He'll tell

my grandmother that we've been roaming the gardens in the dead of night and she'll book us on the next train home. Quick, let's hide on the back of that Land Rover.'

Crouched beneath a dusty tarpaulin, they held their breath as they waited for the footsteps to pass. Next thing they knew a door clicked open. The vehicle rocked slightly as someone climbed in. Martine could have wept with frustration. Of all the rotten luck. She was longing for her bed. Now they were going to be hauled off on some three a.m. errand.

Ben was tense too, waiting for the lights to come on and the engine to start, but the vehicle glided forward in darkness. It was being pushed. Glen and Goodwin wanted to leave the sanctuary unheard and unseen.

For several long minutes the jeep continued its eerie silent journey. Even when the engine started and the vehicle sped up, the driver didn't switch on the lights.

Martine closed her eyes. Foggy tendrils of sleep wafted into her tired brain. Once, they halted, but only to open a gate. The terrain grew rougher. The children were poised to leap off if the smallest opportunity presented itself. None did. Martine whiled away the time trying to dream up imaginative excuses. She'd thought of five when the Land Rover slowed, turned and jerked to a stop. The doors slammed. Boots crunched away.

Ben lifted the tarpaulin. They were in the overgrown yard of a derelict redbrick barn. Inside it, the men had turned on a heavy-duty torch. Light spilled out of the door and fractured roof, revealing a rusting plough smothered in grass. Behind the barn were low-slung hills, silhouetted against a black and blue sky. A line of trees and bushes shielded the building from the road.

'I'm out of bright ideas,' Martine said. 'Any suggestions?'

· 16 ·

'We should come clean now and tell them we're here,' whispered Ben. 'Honesty is usually the best policy. Whatever they're up to, they'll be more cross if they catch us later. 'If we admit that we sneaked out to check on Jabu and it all went wrong, I'm sure Glen will see the funny side.'

Martine wasn't convinced. 'It depends why they're here, doesn't it? People involved in illegal activities tend to have a humour bypass.'

'What makes you think they're doing something illegal? Maybe they're renovating the barn.'

Martine raised an eyebrow. 'At three in the morning?'

'It's unlikely, I know, but they're both so busy that it could be the only time they get to work on it. Glen's a good man. He runs a sanctuary. The chances of him being involved in anything criminal are slim to non-existent . . . What is it?'

'Another vehicle's coming. Ah, now I get it. This is a rendezvous point for a secret meeting.'

Ben stuck his head out to get a better view. 'Whoever it is has their lights turned off too.'

Ducking under the tarpaulin, he tugged it so that it covered them but left a slit through which they could watch the barn. Presently a horsebox lorry reversed up to the barn.

Over the roar of the engine, Ben's sharp ears picked up a faint whirring sound. At first he thought it was coming from the horsebox, but when the ignition was turned off the noise continued. He glanced up. A tiny blue light was tracing a figure of eight over the barn. He tried to make sense of what he was seeing. 'Is there any such thing as a blue firefly?' he asked Martine.

She giggled. 'If they were blue, they wouldn't be called fireflies. They'd be ice flies or something.'

Glen and Goodwin emerged and greeted the lone driver, distracting Ben. Next time he looked the blue dot was gone.

As the men gripped hands, the visitor's face was briefly illuminated. Martine was astonished to recognise Dr Marius Goss, head of the charity FAW (Fight for African Wildlife). He looked exactly as she remembered him from the Breakfast News that New Year's Day morning at Sawubona, except that now there were purple bruises of tiredness beneath his eyes.

'Still think we should pop up and confess we're here?' she whispered as the men disappeared behind the horsebox.

Ben grinned. 'Not a chance. Things have just got interesting.'

'I apologise for putting you in this position but I didn't know where else to turn,' Dr Goss was saying as Glen prepared to lower the horsebox ramp. 'Besides, she knows you. That ought to make handling her easier.'

'It won't make the slightest difference,' Glen said irritably. 'She might have a dim memory of me but if we've done our job right she's truly wild.'

They pulled down the ramp. There was a dragon snort followed by a blur of grey. The men disappeared into the barn and pulled shut the rickety wooden door . . .

'A rhino!' gasped Ben. 'What do you think they're up to?'

'I'm not sure but I intend to find out. Coming?'

Keeping to the shifting shadows, they slipped off the Land Rover and crept behind the barn. There were so many missing bricks, they had no trouble finding peepholes.

A chaotic scene greeted them. A female rhino with the longest horn they'd ever seen was charging blindly round the barn. The tranquiliser had worn off. She was ready to crush and maim anyone she could find.

Goodwin and Dr Goss had chosen the sensible option of watching from behind the remains of a wall. Glen stepped boldly into view. The rhino swung to face him, snorting with rage.

Glen dropped to his knees. He was so close to Ben and Martine that they could have reached though a gap and touched him. He began to breathe a sort of rhino Morse code. Three times he repeated it. He was reassuring the rhino in her own language, telling her she was among friends.

The effect was instantaneous. Her chest still heaved with fear, but she recognised Glen and she was listening. She breathed back a question.

Once more, Glen breathed the same pattern. *Don't be afraid. You're among friends now. You're safe.*

She asked him another question.

Martine's chest was tight with emotion. *He knows the answer,* she thought. *He speaks Rhino.*

Glen breathed and the rhino responded. He breathed again – three long puffs, one short and two medium. Once more the rhino responded. Then he simply held out his arms, as if inviting a child for a hug.

Without warning, the rhino charged at him. Martine was certain that the sanctuary owner was going to be trampled to death before their eyes. But Glen didn't move. He held out his arms and the rhino rushed into them, skidding to a halt. As gently as a kitten, she pressed her wrinkled grey face against his tanned, stubbly one. Her eyes squeezed shut. A single tear slid down a groove in her cheek.

'And that,' said Dr Goss, 'is why I'm prepared to devote my life to saving these special creatures. In my experience, they have the sweetest nature in the animal kingdom.'

'That's what I tell our new volunteers,' agreed Goodwin. 'Every orphan we get at Golden Gate is traumatised. They've witnessed their mum being maimed or killed. There have been gunshots, helicopters or even grenades. Take Honey here. She was petrified and full of rage when she came to us as a two-month-old baby. In the first weeks, she charged us so many times we lost count. But once she understood that we were trying to help her, she was the same as every other orphan we've had – as loving as the best cat or dog. Or perhaps we should say the best horse. Rhinos have a similar character to horses.'

Glen stood up slowly, rubbing Honey behind her ears to keep her calm. 'Which brings us to the question of what we do next. It'll be light soon. Marius, I have to admit that I'm deeply unhappy that you've brought Honey here. I know we were the ones who raised her, but my understanding was that she was living successfully in the wild on the reserve at Mpumalanga. Our sanctuary has never been a target for poachers. I'd hate for that to change.'

Dr Goss moved cautiously out from behind the partition. 'I'm sorry. As I explained, it was an emergency. Despite being sworn to secrecy, a visitor to the Mpumalanga reserve recently blogged that Honey had been confirmed as having the longest horn of any rhino in South Africa. It's nearly 1.6 metres long, worth hundreds of thousands of dollars to poachers. Some local media picked up the story. At FAW, we've now had reliable intelligence that Honey is the Number One most wanted rhino in South Africa. Every poacher in the country is after her.'

'But what do you expect us to do here?' demanded Glen. 'We have limited security and these days poachers have automatic weapons. It's a war. Game reserves have become battlegrounds. We've chosen the barn as a hiding place for Honey because it's on a disused road with few passers-by. Even so, it's only a matter of time before someone witnesses us coming and going and gets curious. How are we going to fence the place? Honey can't live in the barn, she'll go crazy.'

Dr Goss was unruffled. 'There's something I didn't mention on the phone. We have a slight problem.'

'Just the one,' Glen said with heavy sarcasm.

'Three days ago, Honey gave birth to a calf. It was stillborn, but she's been broken-hearted and searching for it ever since. She'll need a companion to keep her calm.'

'The goat?' Goodwin suggested.

Glen stroked rhino's head. 'Marius, you haven't answered my question. What happens next? The best that I can offer is one security guard. It'll mean leaving the sanctuary unguarded at night so you'll to have to come up with another solution and fast. We might be able to keep Honey safe for a few days or maybe a week, but sooner or later the hunters are going to find her. I don't want that on my conscience.'

Martine felt for Dr Goss. He looked shattered.

'Glen, give us forty-eight hours to find a solution. My friends at FAW are pulling out all the stops to find Honey a forever home. We'll make a plan.'

'I can't think what's eating Glen this morning,' moaned Carlos, as he dished up pecan nut pancakes with maple syrup. 'He's being a beast. Those greedy baboons have trashed my vegetable patch *yet again*. When I asked what he was planning to do about it, I got zero sympathy. He told me that if the extent of my problems in life were a few missing carrots, I should consider myself a fortunate man.'

If they'd had the energy, Martine and Ben would have laughed. Earlier, they'd bumped into Susie. She'd also laid the blame for her wrecked garden on a troop of baboons with a reputation for destruction.

'If I see them again, I'll blast them with my paintball gun. Oh, don't fret. It stings, but does them no harm whatsoever. Teaches them a lesson, though!'

The real culprits were the picture of innocence.

'Partners in crime,' said Martine as they watched Jabu and Billy play rodeo games after breakfast.

Ben covered his mouth to hide a yawn. He'd had to spring out of bed at five a.m. to groom horses after less than an hour's sleep. Martine counted herself fortunate to have managed two and a half.

'Morning, kids,' Victor said brightly. 'Something's come up and I have to return to Pretoria earlier than expected. I wanted to say goodbye. Apologies for being like a bear with a sore head yesterday, Martine. I'm stressed about exams but that's no excuse. Enjoy the rest of your stay. Hope Jabu makes a full recovery.'

'Hey, Victor, did you manage to fix it?' Martine called as he walked away.

He turned, pinning his glasses to the bridge of his nose. 'Fix what?'

'Your drone. Did you figure out what was wrong with it?'

'Oh, that. Nah, I was up half the night fiddling with it but it's broken beyond repair. I'm going to tell my professor that I can't be involved in the project. Too time-consuming. I need to focus on my studies.'

'What's a drone got to do with veterinary medicine?' asked Ben when Victor was out of earshot.

Martine leaned over the gate and scratched Billy between the horns. The goat's white eyelashes fluttered in ecstasy. 'That's what I asked. His university is developing drones with infrared cameras that can patrol game reserves at night and alert rangers if poachers are about. They look like mini-helicopters. I think it's a brilliant idea. Victor seemed quite excited about it, but I suppose he was fed up with trying to repair the drone. He's under a lot of pressure to get his degree. The hopes of the village are riding on him.'

'Hey, guys, I've been looking everywhere for you,' said Jean-Pierre, one of the French volunteers, coming up to them with a smile. 'Today I'm going to teach you how to massage a baby rhino.'

Midnight found them hard at work on Operation Rhino, revived by a nap. It had been a blazing blue day, dripping with humidity. In the Rhino Nursery, all nine orphans had crowded into the wallow. Martine and Ben used a hose to cool down Jabu and Billy – and each other.

At lunchtime, Susie had insisted that all staff and volunteers take the afternoon off. The drooping children needed no second invitation. They headed straight for the hammock they'd spied in a deliciously cool grove of Lombardi poplar trees. Soothed by a fountain, they were asleep in an instant.

Dinner that evening was a barbecue, known in South Africa as a *braai*. Chef Carlos served up potatoes baked in the coals, vegetarian and fish kebabs, charred sweetcorn and Greek salad. Somehow Ben and Martine managed to find a corner for dessert: homemade vanilla and ginger ice cream.

Midway through the evening Susie received a phone call to say that her mum, who lived near Johannesburg, was unwell. She and Glen packed an overnight bag and set off at once. Martine wondered if Goodwin would be taking care of Honey. It was a big job for one man.

By ten-thirty p.m., Amelia was snoring softly. Martine and Ben were down in the living room, working their way through the Stars and Stripes guest list.

'Is there anything particular that I should be searching for?' asked Ben.

'That's just it, we don't know,' said Martine. 'Anything could be relevant and nothing could be relevant. We're groping in the dark. Trust your instincts. If something doesn't feel right, it probably isn't. Look for connections too. If one of the guests had an accomplice, they might have pretended not to know each other.'

She logged on to the Internet. 'I'm going through websites and social media stuff. So far everyone appears to be pretty ordinary. The surfers' Facebook pages are what you'd expect – hundreds of beach pictures and videos of them riding tubes. I found two articles on An, the dancer. She's famous in Vietnam but from what I can tell she leads a quiet life and spends her spare time gardening. Her uncle has been like a father to her.'

Martine scrolled down the list of names. 'That's as far as I've got. Mr Chan was my chief suspect, but if he is a rhino horn smuggler he does a good job of hiding it. He works in insurance and plays golf. Doesn't mean he's not a criminal but there's no evidence that he is.'

Ben picked up a pen. 'Perhaps we're going about this the wrong way. What if we wrote our gut feelings about each person beside the names?'

A wave of shame washed over Martine as she recalled giving Jayden the rhino's location. How much longer could she hide the truth from Ben?

'Why don't you say what you really mean?' she said, covering her guilt with anger. 'You want me to admit that I behaved like an idiot groupie over the Take Flight boys, don't you?'

She switched off the PC and jumped up to go.

Ben was startled. 'Martine, wait. That's not what I meant at all. What I was trying to say was, "What if we linked the dry bits of information with random stuff we saw or had a funny feeling about on the night. I'll use Mr Chan as an example. Please, sit down. Pleeaase.'

Martine did as he asked and grudgingly rebooted the computer. Ben read over her shoulder.

'All right, what you've learned about Mr Chan is that he's thirty-nine and works as an accountant for Aquarius Home Insurance in Hong Kong. He and his wife have one son. He plays golf at the Royal Hong Kong Golf Club. We don't have any information on Mrs Chan, except that they've been married for eight years. That's all pretty dull.

'But if we add in our observations about the safari, things get more interesting. Tendai told me that Mr Chan got really agitated when Liam suggested injecting rhino horn with poison to stop people buying it. Then, at the dinner, I overheard him telling Thomas, the new game ranger, that his wife was suffering from terrible migraines because they'd run out of her Chinese medicine. He was desperate to get hold of it. He said he'd pay any price.

'Thomas told him that the pharmacy in Storm Crossing stocked migraine tablets but Mr Chan wasn't interested. He said Western medicine couldn't fix what was wrong with her. Later, I saw Thomas write something on a bit of paper and give it to him. What if they were making a deal to contact a poacher for powdered rhino horn, with Thomas getting a cut of the fee?'

Martine had recovered enough to be impressed. 'That's ace detective work, Ben. Sorry I blew up. It's been a tough week and I'm over-tired and over-sensitive.'

Ben was so happy that she was no longer mad at him he could have hugged her, but that would have been weird. All he said was: 'It's fine. If I'd seen Cleo and Spartacus after the poachers had finished with them, I'd be a wreck. Don't worry, Martine. We're going to track down the monsters who destroyed them even if it takes us ten years.'

He looked at his watch. 'We should get some sleep soon. How about checking out one more guest before we crash? Have a look at my list of names. Did you hear any interesting snippets of conversation or see any of them behaving oddly?'

Martine took a deep breath. 'Yes, I did. Before we left for the game drive, I saw Jayden and his manager having a row under the mango trees. Later, Jayden gave Dirk what sounded like a warning. He told him he needed to "fix" what he'd done before it was too late. He added: "If you don't, *I* will."' Dirk was livid. He said something nasty about Jayden's fifteen seconds of fame almost being up.'

Ben leaned forward. 'Any idea what they might have been arguing about?'

'None at all, but a lot of arguments seem to be about power, love or money. I doubt power or love have anything to do with it. That leaves money.'

'Interesting,' said Ben thoughtfully. He glanced at his own notes. 'I'm sure you know everything there is to know about Jayden, Liam and Lachlan, so I'll tell you what I've found on Dirk. Born in Devon in the UK, the oldest son of a trawlerman. Joined the Navy but was discharged after he was mugged and almost killed in an alleyway in Saigon. A stranger saved his life. He was down to his last five pounds when he found a job on a cruise ship. Worked his way up to Entertainment Director. Discovered Jayden busking in the rain on a street corner in Exeter. Persuaded two *X-Factor* rejects to join them. The rest is history.'

Martine stretched wearily. 'Did you read about their tattoos?'

Ben grinned. 'No, I skipped that bit. On purpose.'

'The man who saved Dirk's life had a tattoo of a koi on his arm. Koi are those oriental fish that resemble goldfish, only they're much larger and look as if they've been hand-painted in watercolour. According to Chinese legend, if a koi succeeds in climbing the waterfall at Dragon Gate on the Yellow River, it becomes a dragon. In Asian culture, five golden koi symbolise eternal wealth and health.'

Ben smothered a yawn. 'That's fascinating, but how does it help us?'

'I'm not sure. After Dirk recovered from the knife attack, he had a koi tattooed on his arm as a tribute to the man who saved him. When he started managing the band, the boys decided that they should each get one too.'

Ben sat up, suddenly interested. 'So there are five golden koi tattoos, signifying eternal wealth and health?'

There was a pause as Martine digested this. The koi story was so familiar to her that it hadn't for a second occurred to her that it might somehow be significant.

'Let's say you're right and that money was the cause of the argument between Jayden and Dirk,' said Ben. 'Dirk could be in financial trouble. That could be a motive for selling rhino horn. I'll take a look at Take Flight's blog and their Facebook and Twitter pages. There may be a clue there.'

There was a knock at the door. Martine started in fright, but was grateful for the distraction. The last thing she wanted was for Ben to stumble across Jayden's Tweet.

Ben padded to the spyhole on bare feet. 'I think it's that girl,' he said under his breath. 'The one who borrowed your book.'

Martine flew to the door and unlocked it.

Saf was on the doorstep, scruffy as a stray left on the mat. 'Sorry to bother you so late. I saw your light on and thought you'd want to know that your rhino has escaped.'

'Which rhino?' In her tiredness, Martine's mind leaped to Honey. Had Dr Goss whisked Honey away to another safe house? Then she remembered that the girl didn't know about the rhino with the record-breaking horn. Nobody did.

'*Your* rhino,' Saf said impatiently. 'Jabulani. Goodwin took away his goat friend and I think he got lonely. There's a hole in the fence. Ex-fence, should I say. Now it resembles an exploded diagram. Anyway, he's gone.'

· 18 ·

Ben shone a torch at the chaos of tracks outside Jabu's enclosure. He had no trouble identifying the rhino's. Despite his bulk, the orphan had dainty feet. His rigid toes left prints the shape of a three-leafed clover.

'The main gates are locked at night so he can't have gone far,' said Ben. 'He'll be making friends with the babies in the nursery or destroying what's left of Chef Carlos's vegetable patch. We've rounded him up before. I'm sure we can do it again, especially now there's three of us.'

Saf squirmed and looked at her shoes, once-white sneakers polka-dotted with mulberry juice. 'It might not

131

be as easy as that. See, an ignoramus might have left the gate open by mistake.'

'How could any ignoramus have been so ignorant?' cried Martine in annoyance.

'Because she was so hungry that all she could think about was the food Carlos had left for her on the kitchen windowsill.'

'The chef puts food out for . . . for the ignoramus?'

Saf kicked a stone and scowled. 'Why are we wasting time talking? Your rhino calf could be in Lesotho by now.'

'She's right,' said Ben. 'He could.'

He resumed his careful study of Jabu's spoor. Apart from a short detour to gobble a succulent plant, the rhino had trotted directly to the gate.

Martine watched the arc of Ben's torch sweep the gravel road.

'He's an apprentice tracker at Sawubona, my grandmother's game reserve in the Cape' she told Saf proudly.

The girl was unimpressed. 'Pity he's not a professional.'

'He's better than a lot of professionals,' Martine said loyally. 'Our warden, Tendai, teaches him San Bushman techniques. He says that Ben was born with a tracker's intuition. That's not something you can learn; it has to be inside you.'

Ben jogged back to them. 'Unfortunately, Jabulani's had a head start of at least an hour, possibly because the ignoramus was tucking into dinner . . . '

'And reading a book,' admitted Saf, shame-faced.

'He's moving too fast for us to catch him on foot. We don't know the area and anything could happen – probably bad. I'll fetch one of the ponies. We'll cover more ground on horseback and we can escape if we run into trouble. Martine, you might want to bring along your survival kit in case he's hurt. Grab some of those coconut bars to eat too. Who knows how long we'll be out there.'

Saf's eyes flashed with excitement. 'I'll come too. Nobody knows the Golden Gate Highlands better than me.'

'Thanks for the offer, but we can only take one horse,' said Ben. 'We'll have to go on our own. Besides, it's one in the morning. Shouldn't you be in bed?'

'Shouldn't you?' she retorted. 'Whatever. Like I haven't got better things to do than go hunting for a rhino in the dark in an area crawling with rhinkhals. It's not as if I have a death wish or anything.'

'Rhinkhals?' Martine said nervously. 'What are rhinkhals?'

'Ring-necked spitting cobras. There are tons of them about, but don't panic. The furthest they can spray venon is about two and a half metres. Provided you don't step on one, you'll be fine. Goodnight!'

They rode bareback, flying through the night like outlaws in a Western. Martine had pleaded with Ben to saddle Tau, the Basotho pony, but there was no time.

'If there are two people, this is a much more comfortable way to ride,' Ben assured her. 'Saddles are designed for one person.'

'But what if I slip off?'

'You'll be holding on to me and I have no intention of slipping off. Martine Allen, get a grip. Tau is barely fourteen hands high. Your usual ride is a giraffe and he's like a skyscraper in comparison. There are Olympic eventers you couldn't pay enough to climb onto Jemmy. They'd be shaking in their long boots.'

'Okay, okay, you've made your point,' said Martine, clinging tightly to his waist. 'By the way, I left a note for Amelia in case she wakes up and finds us missing. If we're home before she gets up, I'll tear it up. It might be better to pretend this never happened.'

Martine had expected the search for Jabu to be a slow creep through the dark as Ben hunted for crushed ants' nests, nibbled grass or any other sign of the rhino's passing. But they'd set off at a canter and barely slowed. He'd explained his theory as they went.

'You know about infrasound, right?'

As it happened, Martine did. She'd done a school project on it after she and Ben were saved by dolphins in the Bazaruto Islands of Mozambique. The lowest frequency a human ear can detect is 20 hertz. Anything lower than that is called infrasound. The few species of animals able to detect it are able to communicate across enormous distances. Researching her project, Martine had discovered that Blue and baleen whales produced sounds and songs that ranged from 10 hertz to 31 hertz.

Their messages to pods located hundreds of kilometres across the ocean were as quick and effective as texting.

Elephant infrasound was even more incredible, measuring 15 hertz to 35 hertz. It had blown Martine's mind to learn that it could travel over mountain ranges and forests and be sensed by herds more than ten kilometres away, using only their feet. Other animals that used infrasound were crocodiles, giraffes and okapi. But what Martine hadn't known until now was that rhinos were among the kings of infrasound, picking up sounds between 5 and 75 hertz.

'This might sound far-fetched,' said Ben, 'but I believe that Jabu's on his way to the barn where Honey's being hidden.'

'You think they've talked to each other using infrasound?'

'Either that or he was using it to try to find Billy. It's worth a shot, isn't it? We've got two choices. Either we wait until morning, by which time Jabu might have got lost or hurt himself, or we act on a hunch. We know that Goodwin suggested putting the goat in with Honey to keep her company. What if Jabu heard his friend bleating in distress as he was driven to the barn? He breaks out of his pen and trots off to help him. As he gets nearer, he realises that Billy's with another rhino – a mum like the one Jabu lost.'

Martine's heart clenched with almost unbearable longing. If only her ears were good enough to hear infrasound. Maybe then she'd be able to communicate with the mother *she'd* lost.

Ben eased Tau to a walk. By taking a direct route through the bush, they'd shaved at least a kilometre off their journey. Now they were on the unmade road. By Martine's reckoning, they were five minutes' ride from the barn. She couldn't wait to get off. Her bum was killing her.

When they reached the entrance to the overgrown yard, Ben tethered Tau in the trees and gave him a couple of carrots. 'What are we going to say to whoever is guarding Honey?' he asked Martine.

'We'll tell the truth, or something like it. We can say that we were worried that Jabu might be run down by a car if we didn't try to find him right away so we headed in the general direction of his tracks. They brought us here. We'll be in huge trouble for not waking the grown-ups, but that's nothing new.'

He grinned. 'True. Of course, I could be totally wrong about which way Jabu went. Right at this minute, he might be fast asleep in Chef's vegetable patch.'

He switched on his torch and called out loudly as they approached the barn. 'The last thing we want is to be shot by the guard by accident,' he whispered.

But the barn was in darkness. Nothing and no one moved in the yard. Martine's skin crawled with nerves. Something wasn't right.

They found Jabu at the back of the ruin, his nose pressed to the peepholes. He was exchanging breaths with the goat and with Honey. He was so pleased to see Martine he almost bowled her over.

While she distracted him, Ben searched for the guard.

It didn't take long. He was slumped against a tree, unconscious.

Ben glanced at the flask beside him. 'Drunk on the job. Good thing Glen's not here. He'd be furious.'

'Not drunk, drugged,' said Martine, tipping out the remaining liquid and showing Ben the tell-tale grains of white.

They stared at the gritty puddle on the grass. It could mean only one thing: the poachers were on their way.

'What are we going to do?' whispered Martine in panic. 'We can't abandon the animals. They'll be slaughtered.'

'If we stay, *we* might be slaughtered,' was Ben's chilling response.

'You go,' said Martine. 'I'm not leaving them to be shot in cold blood. I want to at least try to move them.'

'A five-ton rhino, a massive orphan and a goat with horns? What do you suggest, that we tie them to Tau and gallop back to the sanctuary?'

'Let's free them,' said Martine. 'If Honey can run, she has a chance. It might be a one per cent chance, but it's better than being a sitting duck.'

The first thing Ben did was release the pony. 'Tau's the least of our problems. As soon as I let him go, he'll gallop back to the sanctuary. With any luck, someone will hear him. They'll realise we're missing and raise the alarm. Until then, we're on our own.'

They sprinted to the barn. The padlock had been broken off the door, another sign that the poachers were close. Despite this, they moved slowly and carefully, not wanting to alarm Honey until they'd persuaded her out into the open.

They didn't notice Jabu until he barged between them. When he saw Honey, his lily-pad ears flapped forward. He squeaked madly. It was as if he was saying, 'Mum! Mum!'

He rushed at her with such enthusiasm that the goat had to leap out of the way to avoid being crushed. The feeling wasn't mutual. Honey looked down her nose at the calf. He was an imposter, not her own baby. She stamped a foot and threatened to spear him with her long horn. Billy rushed to defend his friend, David against Goliath, slashing at her with his own tiny horns.

'Perfect,' Ben said drily. 'When the hunters arrive, their job might already be done. These three will have gored each other to death.'

Martine was desperate. 'What are we going to do?'

Jabu had retreated to a corner to sulk. Contrasted with Honey, he looked small and vulnerable. When Billy tried nuzzling him, he sank miserably to the ground.

'Martine, we've run out of time,' said Ben. 'We have to go. We can leave the door open and Honey will have to fend for herself. We can't move an angry adult rhino. We'd be more likely to be killed by her than by the poachers. Let's attach that bit of rope to Billy's collar and lead him away. Hopefully, Jabu will get up and follow. We might be able to save two out of three.'

'Ben, wait. I think Honey's had a change of heart.'

The mother rhino began to croon a rhino lullaby. To Martine's ears, it resembled a whale song. Jabu didn't raise his head, but Honey didn't give up. She blew and crooned some more. Using her horn, she gently lifted him to his feet. As he stood trembling, she guided him round to her flank. Then he understood. Her own calf had died so recently she still had milk. It wasn't long before he was drinking greedily. Honey gave a shuddering rhino sigh.

Through the stillness of the night came the *whup, whup, whup* of an approaching helicopter. The children ran to the door. It was a distant speck but it was on its way.

Ben lashed the rope to goat's collar. 'Keep to the trees, Martine. The National Park is on the other side of that hill. If we can make it there, they might not dare to come after us. Let's run and hope that Jabu follows.'

He slapped Honey lightly on the rump. She bolted out of the barn, reaching the trees just as a helicopter came roaring over the top of them. Torn between following her or the goat, Jabu chose his friend now being dragged, protesting, after Ben. Honey plunged after them, determined not to lose her newly adopted son. Martine joined the chase. Incredibly, all five of them were running in the same direction.

The helicopter had its lights off and the poachers on board hadn't yet seen them. As it came in to land, the barn was illuminated. Four men jumped out. When Martine glanced over her shoulder, they were rushing back and forth like angry termites outside the empty ruin.

The helicopter wobbled into the air again. It raked the trees with a searchlight. The children and animals were spotted in minutes.

'Faster!' yelled Ben, but it was no use. Martine had a stitch and Jabu was exhausted. Grit and bits of bark stung their faces as the helicopter hovered overhead, one of the men leaning out with a semi-automatic weapon in his hands.

They fled into a thicket. Thorns and sticks tore at their limbs and clothes. Just when Martine thought things couldn't get any worse, they did. Bursting from the trees, they found their path blocked by a high fence topped with barbed wire. On the other side was the Golden Gate Highlands National Park. They were trapped!

The pilot was searching for a level place to land. The helicopter's machine-gun roar and the down-draft of its blades sent the animals wild with terror.

Out of the blackness flew an apparition. 'This way,' yelled Saf. 'There's nowhere for them to land. They'll need to return to the barn. We'll have a head start.'

Dumbly, they stumbled after her. Billy followed Jabu, who was followed by Honey. Martine was breathless with fear, her lungs bursting. Saf guided them to a gate, to which she had a key. As soon as they were through it, she locked it behind them.

'I can't go on,' gasped Martine, and neither can Jabu. We'll stay behind. The poachers are not going to hurt a girl and a baby rhino. It's Honey they're after.'

'You can go on and you will,' said Saf, pulling her to her feet. Honey clearly felt the same about Jabu because she prodded him with her horn. 'We're going together or not at all. Now move.'

A shot rang out. The men had reached the gate and

were furious to find it locked. More shots followed. Martine discovered that few things were more energising than flying bullets.

After slipping and sliding into a gulley, she followed the others along an old stream bed, deep enough to conceal them from view. Unable to switch on a torch, the humans made slow progress, tripping over roots and stones in the dark. The animals had no difficulty at all.

They're super-beings compared to us, thought Martine. *Bionic.*

Ben rounded the bend up front with Billy. 'It's a dead end,' he shouted despairingly.

The helicopter was rising into the sky again. It was heading their way. *It's over,* thought Martine. *It's really over. We're out of options.*

She hadn't counted on Saf behaving like a superhero herself. Dashing past Ben, she peeled back the rock with her bare hands. Or so it seemed. In reality, a photograph printed on durable fabric created an optical illusion. Behind it was a yawning black hole. The weary menagerie trooped in. The cloth dropped down. They were safe and alive.

For now.

19

'It was Pa's idea,' said Saf. 'He was a member of the paleontology team that discovered the oldest dinosaur embryos on earth at Golden Gate back in the late seventies. This is one of the few pictures I have of him.'

She handed them a black and white photo in an antique frame. 'He's the one in the middle wearing the bush hat and the grin. My favourite memories are watching him type up his notes on digs. Most kids would find that numbingly boring, right? Not me. Non-paleontologists think of a handful of dust as dirt and worms. I see it as living history. What I love about this park is that every bucket of dirt potentially contains specks of fossilised plants or eggs from the Triassic Period. That's nearly 200 million years ago. It might have fragments of *Massospondus* bones or a couple of teeth from a *Thecodontia* . . . Uh, where was I?'

'You were saying that this cave was your dad's idea,' Ben prompted.

She grinned. 'Oh, yeah. After my mum ran off with a jazz musician – which, to be honest, was fine by me since she didn't seem particularly fond of us – Pa and me spent more and more time here. He was home-schooling me so it's not like I had to be in class or anything. We found this place when we were trying to shelter from a hailstorm. I said jokingly to Pa, "Wouldn't it be nice if we lived here and didn't have to bother driving to and from the village ten times a day?"

'The best thing about Pa was that he loved mad ideas. The more bonkers they were, the more he liked them. He wasn't like a real grown-up at all. Right then, he said, "Saf, that's the finest plan I've heard in at least an hour. Let's do it. Let's start moving in tomorrow. It can be our second home." We took a photo of a rock face, had it printed on waterproof cloth and that became our door.'

Martine sipped her *boontjiesgras* (bean grass) tea and gazed around the cave. It was more homely than most houses she'd visited. There were two sections to it. On ground level was a larger cave striped with rust from ancient storms. The ceiling had the vaulted appearance of a cathedral. Last time she'd looked, Jabu had been helping himself to more milk from Honey, and Billy had been chewing contentedly on a midnight feast of dried corn and a straw hat.

A second cloth hid the entrance to a narrow tunnel. Steep and slippery rock stairs led to a smaller cave. It was in here that Saf and her dad had created the cosy den they now occupied. Every time one of them moved, shadows danced across the walls like living cave-paintings.

Martine was enraptured. She could have moved in at once. On the cave floor were two mattresses and a beanbag, each covered with Basotho blankets in burgundy and red. Beside a small desk and chair was a shelf crafted from a piece of driftwood. It housed books on everything from herbal medicine to Triassic monsters. *The Ghost Ship Mystery* had pride of place.

There was even a mini kitchen. What surprised Martine was how neat and clean everything was. Sacks of dried beans and rice and cans of Chakalaka and condensed milk were stored in traditional baskets. Two charred pots swung from wooden pegs driven into a crevice. A portable gas stove sat beside a bucket of water. A broom made of tightly bound twigs was propped in one corner.

It was a deeply personal space, put together with love. Having lived through the desolation of grief, Martine knew well how lonely Saf must feel. 'You must miss your pa dreadfully,' she said, a catch in her voice.

Saf shook her head. 'Not when I'm here. When I'm in the cave, it still feels as if he's with me. He'd sit at his desk reading and making notes in microscopic handwriting, sometimes till dawn. He worked so hard. It's almost as if he knew he wouldn't be around for much longer and he wanted to do as much research and leave as much information as he possibly could. Tried to teach me as much as he could too. Fat lot of use that was.'

She rubbed her eyes fiercely. 'He'd be ashamed of me now. A truant thief in rags, that's me. I've failed every exam this year.'

Ben sat up on the beanbag. 'Ashamed? You're kidding, aren't you? Tonight you've saved the lives of two clueless kids; a goat; a skinny orphan rhino who, if we ever get out of this mess, will one day be a mighty bull, and a female Southern White Rhino with the longest horn in South Africa.'

Saf gaped. 'Ah, that explains why they want her so desperately; they can smell gold. Mmm, I had a feeling I was gonna regret coming after you on my bike. I was worried you might get mugged by bandits or something. I'd have been safer poking at a hornets' nest with a sizzling stick of dynamite.'

She fixed them with a challenging stare. 'We can talk in circles for hours but I think you owe me the truth. Or is it a giant coincidence that you went out looking for Jabu and just happened to find yourselves rescuing a totally different rhino with a world record-breaking horn from a gang of trigger-happy lunatics in a helicopter?'

'It's a long story,' admitted Martine.

Saf's white teeth sparkled in the candlelight. 'We have all night. I'm in no rush to go anywhere, not with the poachers on the prowl. Are you?'

By now it was nearly two in the morning and the Basotho blankets were beckoning. It was only because they felt honour-bound to give their rescuer a proper explanation that Martine and Ben told their story, in voices thick with tiredness.

Last but not least, they recalled the *sangoma's* warning on the train and her grandfather's theory if you stared at a man with gold lust hard enough, you could see a worm's evil eyes glowing blood-red at the back of theirs.

'Grace says that, for poachers, rhino horn is the new gold,' said Martine. 'It causes the same sickness. She told us that if we recognised it in any man, woman, boy or girl, we shouldn't stand in their way. We should run.'

'Based on recent experience, that's sound advice,' commented Saf.

She was silent for a moment. 'Do you think the two attacks are linked – the one at Sawubona and the one last night? Could the same people be responsible for both?'

'Until we've narrowed down our list of suspects, it's impossible to say,' answered Ben. 'At the moment Operation Rhino is like a scene from the end of an Agatha Christie film. Ten people are gathered in the drawing room and Poirot is explaining how each one of them has a motive for murdering the butler. Only he'd have solved the mystery by now. We don't have a clue.'

'Agatha *who*?' asked Saf. 'I've seen one film in my life and that was *Jurassic World*, which was cool but messed up all the science. Never mind, I know what you mean. Look, sometimes it helps to have an outside opinion. I spent years helping Pa with his research. You could tell me what you've found so far and I'll see if I can spot anything that doesn't add up.'

'Sure,' said Martine without enthusiasm. She cast a covert glance at Ben. Operation Rhino was their baby. She was reluctant to let anyone else take over. At the same time, a fresh pair of eyes might give them a breakthrough.

'What's weird is that the mission to save Honey was top secret and happened at short notice,' said Ben. 'Only a few trusted people were in on it. So how did the poachers manage to track her down so quickly?'

'My brain hurts,' said Martine. 'So does every millimetre of my body. How about drawing straws for the beds and we can continue this discussion in the morning?'

'Good thinking,' yawned Saf.

'You girls can take the beds,' Ben said tiredly. 'I'm fine on the beanbag. I'd be happy with a bed of nails if it meant I could shut my eyes.'

Saf tossed him a blanket. 'Sleep as long as you need to. Tomorrow we'll have to work out where to move to and how to get help. We can't be here when night falls. The poachers will be back and they'll bring reinforcements.'

There was no reply from Ben. He was dead to the world.

Saf and Martine checked on the animals one last time. The crash of rhinos had crashed. Billy was nestled amid the tangle of grey limbs. None of the animals stirred as the torchlight slid over them.

'I've never been close to a fully grown rhino,' Saf said in wonder. 'Honey's face is so innocent. She's like an armour-plated angel.'

Martine smiled. 'She is. Hard to believe that there are people in this world so greedy or superstitious that they'd destroy her for a horn that has no more power to cure disease than my fingernails. The ancestors of the African Rhino roamed the planet for sixty million years. The Tibetan Woolly Rhino survived an Ice Age! It's scary to think that modern rhinos could be extinct by the time we leave school.'

Up in the den, Saf snuggled beneath her blanket. 'Pa often told me that people make the mistake of thinking that paleontology is about the past when really it's about learning from the past to make a better future. What happened tonight made me think about his words. If I get a second chance at life, I'm going to make Pa proud. No rhino's going to die on my watch – not if I have anything to do with it.'

In her dreams, Martine murmured: 'Me neither – and that's a promise.'

20

'I refuse to waste police resources on a goat,' said Duty Sergeant Mosaka. 'Trust me, if somebody stole the beast for last night's curry, the evidence has already been devoured.'

Glen tried not to lose his temper. He'd once read an article on mindfulness. It claimed that in times of great stress focusing on a single toe could be beneficial. He attempted that now without success.

'I mentioned Billy because instinct tells me he holds the key to the whole mystery. Naturally, I have no way of knowing whether the goat, kids and rhino are in the same place, or if the kids have been snatched and

Billy is the victim of a hungry villager, or . . . '

'Or vice versa,' he almost added, so addled was his brain. He'd not slept. Having driven for hours to be at the bedside of Susie's sick mother, they'd arrived to find her in perfect health. Oddly, no one at the retirement home would admit to having made the call to say she was ill. At the time, Glen had been so relieved that he'd put it down to a miscommunication. It was only when he and Susie had returned to the sanctuary to find all hell breaking loose that it had occurred to him that the call had been a hoax. Someone had wanted him out of the way.

DS Mosaka turned to a fresh page in his notebook. 'Now you're saying that there are three children missing, not two? No wonder they're missing if you cannot keep count, Mr Lowe. Describe this Billy. Does he have a middle name?'

'Billy's the goat,' said Glen through gritted teeth.

'The goat again!'

'Yes, as I keep explaining, we'd temporarily put him in the barn on Bearded Vulture road. Jabulani adored him. Rhino can communicate across huge distances. If he broke out of his pen because he was pining for Billy, that's where he might have gone. We know from Martine's note that she and Ben went out searching for the rhino calf. It's possible that they tried to follow him.'

'In the middle of the night?'

'It seems that rather than waking Goodwin or one of our volunteers, they took matters into their own hands.'

'You didn't warn them about the perils of venturing out at night in an area where miscreants have been known to operate?' DS Mosaka demanded disapprovingly.

'I didn't get the chance. They'd barely been at the sanctuary for two days. Recently, a couple of rhino were poached at Martine's grandmother's game reserve in the Eastern Cape. The children came to Golden Gate partly to deliver an orphaned calf but also because they were deeply distressed about what had happened on Sawubona. It was Gwyn Thomas's hope that visiting a baby rhino sanctuary would be a healing experience for them.'

Glen tugged miserably at his beard. 'I haven't broken the news to her that they're missing. I wanted to speak to you first. I keep hoping that it's all a bad dream. Amelia, the volunteer who's sharing a cottage with them, is devastated. She slept through everything. This morning she got up and went about her chores, thinking they were having a lie-in. It wasn't until after nine a.m. that she found Martine's note.'

The policeman tipped back his chair and shook his pen at Glen. '*Gogo* is not going to be happy with you, Mr Lowe. Losing one child is bad. Losing two children, plus a goat and rhino – all in the same evening – is plain carelessness.'

Yes, but what are you going to do about it? Glen wanted to scream, but he restrained himself. 'While we're on the subject of missing children, the villagers asked me to report that Sfiso didn't come home last night. It's a common occurrence, but it's yet another coincidence. She's the daughter of the National Park paleontologist who—'

'I'm well aware of Saf,' said DS Mosaka with a grimace. 'We get more complaints about that girl playing truant and "borrowing" things than we do about serial burglars. Her aunt allows the child to run amok. The father was just as irresponsible when he was alive, dragging her around the park to dig up dinosaurs. Leave it to me. I'll contact social services. It's time they took her into care.'

'Don't do that, please . . . '

The policeman righted his chair and drummed five fat fingers on the desk. 'One thing is puzzling me. What was the goat doing in an abandoned barn? It's at least two kilometres from your sanctuary.'

Glen hesitated. Marius would throttle him if he revealed the existence of the rhino with the longest horn in South Africa to a policeman who could easily be corrupt, but what choice did he have?

'We put the goat in the barn to comfort another rhino – an adult female. Her name is Honey.'

DS Mosaka chewed the end of his pen reflectively. 'If I'm not mistaken, your own property is around fifty acres. Could you not have found Honey a corner there? It is a rhino *sanctuary*, is it not?'

'She has a rare infectious disease,' Glen improvised. 'We put her in the barn for safe-keeping. It was a temporary arrangement.'

The policeman made a big show of writing '*DISEASED HONEY PLACED IN RUINED BARN FOR SAFE-KEEPING.*' He underlined the last phrase several times. 'You said "Was".'

'Excuse me?'

'You used the past tense. Let me guess – this rhino has disappeared too?'

'I'm afraid she has.'

'So at the current count, two rhino, three children and a goat vanished from your sanctuary in a single evening when you just happened to be out of town?'

Even to Glen's ears, the conversation had taken a farcical turn. He decided not to mention Victor, who'd not been heard from since setting off to catch a bus to Pretoria the previous morning. 'There is one other thing.'

'Another missing creature? A dog or a cat perhaps? Or is it your wife? Because if she's gone missing, frankly I don't blame her.'

'The children knew each other,' said Glen, ignoring the sarcasm. 'Apparently, Martine had given Saf a mystery novel.'

'A mystery novel?'

'Something about a ghost ship.'

There was a burst of laughter outside the window. DS Mosaka glanced enviously at his colleagues, heading out to lunch. He closed his notebook. 'If that minx Sfiso is with Ben and Martine, I expect she's led them astray. They will be playing games or hiding in a den. One or two of the animals may even be with them. They'll be home when they're hungry. If there's no sign of them by nightfall, feel free to contact me. Until then, sir, I bid you good day.'

The leader of the Python gang of poachers was the type of man who wore mirror sunglasses at night. Rumour had it that he used engine oil to tone his black muscles. Regardless of the weather, he wore combat trousers and a leather jacket decorated with an Army Colonel's insignia. These he'd stolen before being dishonourably discharged from his duties as a soldier in the National Guard.

'Nothing would displease me more than to be outwitted by the Boere Rhino Mafia,' he fumed, referring to the Afrikaans brothers who several years earlier had admitted to killing nineteen rhinos, including calves.

'It was not them, Colonel,' said Tsotsi, who'd led the failed attempt to steal Honey's horn. 'Those Boere tend to have bellies like pregnant women. These people ran very fast.'

'What about the Ferreira Gang or the Congolese? Or perhaps those Mozambican thieves who are in league with the Thai wildlife mafia? What about them? Or are they too busy racketeering and money-laundering these days?'

'I don't think so, Colonel. These poachers were small. I believe they were children.'

'*Children?* Honestly, some of these poachers have no conscience at all. Gone are the days when wildlife trafficking belonged to the criminals. Nowadays there are game ranchers and elements of the South African and Zimbabwean Army muscling in on the rhino horn trade. There are also two judges, nine or ten government officials, wildlife vets, pilots and at least four charity workers that I know of. And that's before we get to the foreigners. Think hard, Tsotsi. Do any of them have kids they could be training to undercut our operation?'

'Unfortunately, it was too dark to see them properly,' said Tsotsi, inching away from the business end of the Colonel's semi-automatic weapon. In his next life, he planned to work in an industry where the boss did not routinely throw tantrums with a beer in one hand and a loaded gun in the other.

As if reading his mind, the Colonel set aside the rifle and picked up a grenade he'd been using as a paperweight. He began to juggle with it. 'Our new informant – how did he say he discovered the rhino with the record-breaking horn?'

Tsotsi took another step back. 'Using a drone, sir. It has night-vision technology and a video camera. He was working late on some university project. While doing a test flight of the drone, he saw her being unloaded by that irritating Dr Goss from FAW. He'd read about her record-breaking horn and he put two and two together. He contacted us via the Dark Web.'

'That was discreet but not discreet enough,' growled the Colonel. 'Some other gang has got wind of our plan. We can still win if we act fast. From what you are telling me, the rhino has escaped into the National Park. We must get to her first, perhaps as early as sunset this evening. It's risky but what can we do. Get in touch with your informant and get him on the case. If he can find the rhino once, he can find her again.'

21

Martine took a sip of the Baobab coffee Ben had brought her and dunked a condensed milk rusk into her mug. Screened from view by a handily placed boulder, they were thawing out in the midday sun. There were many appealing things about cave life, but the shower was not one of them. Saf's dad had rigged up a rainwater tank system beneath an overhanging boulder. It was outdoors, which Martine didn't really mind because there was something freeing about showering while looking out at Echo Ravine, but it was teeth-numbingly cold. It made sense to her now that Saf had dreadlocks and always looked as if she'd been dragged through a protea bush backwards, especially since her aunt's home had no running water.

'*Kgotso, le phelo jwang?*' said Saf, clambering up to join them. Not wanting to be outdone, she'd washed and put on one of her dad's old shirts. It was so long that she'd had to belt it at the waist like a dress.

'What does that mean?' asked Martine.

'It's Sotho for "Peace, how are you?"'

Martine sighed. 'I wish I felt peaceful enough to enjoy this beautiful place, but I can't stop thinking about the poachers. If you hadn't shown up, they'd have murdered us to get at Honey.'

'Probably,' agreed Saf matter-of-factly.

Ben tossed the remains of his rusk to a yellow-breasted pipit. 'What I'd like to know is who betrayed Dr Goss and Glen. Honey was in the barn for seventeen hours in total. The poachers would have needed at least a couple of hours to organise the strike. That leaves a window of around fifteen. Who had the opportunity? A chance passer-by, somebody connected to the sanctuary or a staff member from FAW?'

'There is another possibility,' said Martine. 'As Saf said last night, this attack might in some way be connected to the one at Sawubona. Whoever was responsible for that might have learned that Jabu was being moved to the Golden Gate sanctuary and decided to target some of the older rhino orphans for their mini horns. While they were scouting the area, they might have stumbled across Honey.'

Saf wasn't convinced. 'Sounds a bit far-fetched.'

'If only we had Victor's drone,' said Ben. 'It could be our eyes. We could fly it around the Golden Gate Highlands . . . How big is the park, Saf?'

'Eighty-four thousand acres.'

'We could use the drone to find a safe place for Honey and at the same time track down the poachers.'

Martine choked on her coffee. 'W-what did you say?'

Saf clapped her on the back. 'Are you okay? You look ill.'

'What Ben said about the drone being our eyes. That's how it was done.'

'That's how what was done?' said Ben, not understanding.

'When Victor explained his university project to me, he said the plan was for the drone to whizz around game reserves at night and use its infrared camera to reveal any hunters to the rangers watching it on screen in their office. I thought it was a brilliant idea. But later I realised that if the good guys can use that technology, so can the bad.'

Ben stared at her. 'Are you thinking what I'm thinking?'

'The blue firefly you saw circling the barn wasn't a firefly at all. It was a drone.'

Saf was watching them with interest. 'Do you often do that – read each other's minds?'

Neither heard her.

'That leaves two options,' Ben said. 'Either a poacher just happened to be flying a drone on the particular evening that Honey was delivered, or Victor was lying about his being broken.'

'And why would he lie if he didn't know something?' finished Martine. 'But he's training to be a vet. He's supposed to love animals. Surely he couldn't be behind something so evil. Goodwin would be heartbroken if his nephew was in league with poachers. He has his hopes pinned on Victor to be the first person in the village to graduate.'

'Maybe that's what's gone wrong,' said Ben. 'There's too much pressure on him to succeed. Saf, what do you know about Victor? Martine told me he was horrible to you.'

She grinned. 'He was, but I can't really blame him. I borrowed his Veterinary Dictionary for a month and returned it covered in mulberry stains and pencil markings. I've borrowed other books of his too. But that's not the real reason Victor gets so furious with me. He hates it that I know his weakness.'

Martine put her cup down. 'What weakness?'

'He has a reputation as a hard worker because whenever he's at the sanctuary he's up half the night, supposedly studying. I'm the only one who knows that really he's playing cards on his laptop.'

'You mean Solitaire?' asked Ben. 'There's no harm in that.'

'Not Solitaire, Poker. He likes to gamble.'

'Oh, dear,' said Martine. 'I think we've just found our motive.'

22

If the Cape Vulture riding a thermal above the sandstone cliffs had been less preoccupied with the plump rock hyrax (dassie) it had seen scuttle beneath a boulder, it might have been curious about the eccentric party that marched across the sourgrass veld in the early afternoon sunshine.

It was a Sotho folk-tale that had inspired the children's escape plan. Legend had it that centuries earlier, a monster called *Khodumodumo* had appeared and enslaved the entire Basotho nation, all except one pregnant woman who escaped by camouflaging herself with cow dung and ashes. She was spared because the monster mistook her for a rock. The woman gave birth to a boy who grew into a fine young warrior. He wore a blanket and carried a spear and shield and was known as *Sankatana,* the Ragged-One. *Sankatana* slayed the monster with his spear and freed the captives.

'It's an excellent story, but how does it help us?' asked Martine after Saf had finished relaying it with great theatre.

Saf looked at her as if she'd been absent on the day that brain cells were handed out. 'The poachers will be expecting us to try to escape tonight. They'll be lying in wait. Let's take them off guard by doing it in daylight, using camouflage, like *Sankatana's* mother.'

'How?' asked Ben. 'We can disguise ourselves but we can't exactly conceal a five-ton rhino.'

'Oh, yeah? Watch me.'

A couple of hours later, they set out in procession across the park. Ben was once again leading Billy but the goat was no longer white with chestnut patches. A mix of clay and dung had stained him the colour of the sandstone cliffs.

Jabu had been transformed with charcoal. He was now dark grey and had a stylish black mane, hand-painted with wet soot. He resembled an overweight wildebeest.

But it was Honey whose appearance was most altered. After pouring a bucket of sooty water over her, they'd secured a set of old buffalo horns to her head with string. Saf had wrapped the rhino's own long horn in a brown and green cloth in the hope that from a distance it would not be noticed against the flaxen grass. It was testament

161

to Honey's newfound faith in them that she endured it, albeit grumpily.

'It won't fool anyone on the ground,' said Saf, 'but if the poachers are hunting for Honey in their helicopter or Victor's scouting the reserve with his drone, the last place they're going look is in the middle of a herd of wildebeest.'

They all agreed that if Victor was involved, it would be a mistake to go to the sanctuary for help in case it took time to convince Glen and Goodwin of his guilt. If the student got wind of their discovery, he might vanish from his university lodgings or wherever he'd gone.

Their best hope was Dr Goss. Since they had no phone, it was decided that Saf should hike across the park to the Matlakeng Herbal Trail. The ecologist who conducted tours for visitors had been a close friend of her father's. She trusted him and was sure he'd let her send a message. Her disguise would be a Basotho blanket, the traditional dress of the Sotho people who assisted on the tour.

'I'll tell Aaron that I urgently need to contact Dr Goss. I won't tell him why. He's worked with FAW over issues in the park, so he's bound to have his personal number or know someone who does. I'll send Dr Goss a coded SMS.'

'What will you say?' asked Martine in wonder. Rarely had she met a more resourceful or ingenious girl. Wrapped in a scarlet blanket, Saf seemed to have grown overnight. She carried herself differently. Their mission had given her a reason to live and to fight. She was like the Ragged-One in the legend, a warrior born to slay monsters.

'I'll write: "*In an emergency, the best place to find honey is among the gnus at golden gate. The best place to find friends is brandwag buttress at sundown.*"'

'I'm not sure what any of that means, but it sounds good.'

'It means,' Saf said, 'that if he wants to save his precious rhino and her rescuers, he'll find us hiding in plain sight.'

That afternoon Martine and Ben led Billy and the rhinos to Echo Ravine, where a great herd of wildebeest grazed. They were careful not to venture too close. African gnus are notoriously skittish and the last thing they wanted was to start a stampede. Instead they left the goat and rhinos to do the 'meet and greet' themselves.

'Wildebeests are a bit like cattle,' explained Martine. 'They're inquisitive. If we keep out of the way the gnus will soon wander over to check out this bizarre new species.'

And so it had proved. Within half an hour, the rhinos and a disconcerted Billy had merged with the herd. Without a zoom lens, a casual passer-by would be unlikely to notice them.

Martine was glad to move on. It was a miracle that they'd got the rhinos safely to the cave the night before, and almost as big a feat that they'd persuaded Honey to follow Jabu to Echo Ravine. But the female rhino had grown impatient with being herded around like a sheep. Sooner or later, she'd have rebelled and either attracted the attention of the poachers or sent one or both of the children to hospital. That would have been disastrous.

For now, the rhinos were safe with the wildebeest herd. Ben and Martine's next task was to hike to Brandwag Buttress, where they were meeting Saf at sundown. It was a golden afternoon. As they walked, the landscape unfurled before them. Crumpled emerald slopes and forests of ouhout trees met sandstone cliffs pocked with caves. Deep blue streams overhung with weeping willows bubbled between hills carpeted in alpine grasses.

There were no lions, leopards or elephants in the National Park, but they did see sungazer lizards, grey rhebuck and an oribi, one of the prettiest antelope in Africa. Saf had made them conscious too of beasts unseen. Beneath their feet lay the bones of the Triassic dinosaurs that had once made a kingdom of the Maluti Mountains.

So enchanted was Martine that she briefly forgot why they were there. She'd recognized a wormwood plant by its feathery green leaves and eucalyptus smell. As she launched into an enthusiastic speech about how it cured coughs, flu, earache and loss of appetite, Ben interrupted: 'Martine, we need to concentrate on what we're doing. When we get to the top of Brandwag's Buttress, let's find a place off the beaten track, and go through our suspect list again. If there's a link between what happened here and the attack at Sawubona, we need to find it.'

Martine's heart began to pound steadily, and not because of the climb. So much had happened since they'd galloped out of the sanctuary on Tau that she'd blocked all thoughts of Jayden from her mind. Now they came surging back.

'Sure. Whatever,' she mumbled.

He gave her a puzzled stare, but made no comment. The Brandwag's Buttress route was popular with tourists, particularly at sunset, but the hotel there was closed for renovations and they were hoping they wouldn't run into anyone asking difficult questions. To be on the safe side, Saf had drawn them a map of the path she always took, which was not visible from the hotel or any of the marked routes.

They found the rendezvous point easily. It was a tranquil spot, sheltered from the sun and wind by an overhanging wedge of sandstone. Martine sat on a rock and took a long drink from the water bottle. Her stomach rumbled. Lunch had been raisins and stale nuts. They had a can of condensed milk they were planning to puncture and share for dinner when Saf joined them.

If Saf joins us, said a voice in Martine's head and she shut it out firmly. Saf was smart enough to take care of herself. She'd find the ecologist, send the message and return safely. Very shortly, they'd be rescued.

To take her mind off the doubts that kept crowding into it, Martine focused on the view. Sunset was an hour away but already the sandstone cliffs were tinted a delicate orange.

Ben was using a stick to scratch names in the earth at their feet. 'Let's go through the Stars and Stripes guest list again. There's something we're missing, I'm sure of it.'

'At the moment our main suspects are obvious ones like the Chans,' said Martine. 'They live in Hong Kong, which is one of the top markets for rhino horn, they use Chinese medicine and they had a fit when Liam suggested poisoning rhino horns as a deterrent. But none of those things make them guilty. Why don't we take a hard look at people who seem unlikely, such as the Johnsons?'

'I'll tell you who's even more unlikely,' said Ben. 'An Nzuyen, the Vietnamese ballet dancer. I wonder what was wrong with her uncle. He had a jaundiced look about him, as if he was either recovering from a serious illness or had one. Did you ever find out where he was from?'

'No, but his name cropped up in a couple of articles about An. She grew up in a village in the middle of nowhere and he paid for her to study dance in Saigon.'

Ben went still. 'She trained in Saigon?'

'Mm-hmm.' Martine was hungry and her attention had wandered.

'The same city where Dirk was mugged and almost killed? The city where a stranger saved his life, something that meant so much to him that he had a koi tattooed on his arm as a tribute and inspired the Take Flight boys to do the same?'

'Yes, Saigon,' said Martine. It came out as a croak. In that instant, she saw the whole terrible truth all too clearly, and what she didn't see she could imagine.

Even now, she could picture Dirk and Uncle Huynh smoking in the shadows at the dinner. They'd seemed an odd couple. In fact they were bound by history and destiny. Uncle Huynh had saved Dirk after he was mugged and left for dead. If, decades later, the Vietnamese man fell ill with a life-threatening disease, the manager would have felt honour-bound to return the favour.

Dirk was a wealthy man in his own right, but if Uncle Huynh had no insurance and needed operations or visits to specialists in, say, the US, the medical bills would have been astronomical. If Uncle Huyn's condition continued to worsen, the pair might have resorted to illegal Asian 'cures' such as tiger bones or rhino horn.

Martine suspected that Dirk had been tempted to 'borrow' money from the band's accounts to fund this so-called treatment. Perhaps Jayden had found out about it, which was why he'd told his manager to 'fix' what he'd done. Only Dirk hadn't fixed anything. He'd done something even worse: he'd orchestrated the attack on Sawubona's rhinos, probably using the information in Jayden's Tweet.

She took a deep breath. 'Ben? Ben, there's something I need to tell you.'

It all came out then. How Jayden had laughed away her concerns about telling him the location of the rhinos. How his Tweet had gone viral.

'I knew it.' Ben glared at her, suddenly a stranger. 'I knew you were hiding something. What I didn't know is that you were so starstruck by Jayden Lucas that you'd sacrifice Spartacus and Cleo.'

Tears started pouring down Martine's face. 'It wasn't like that. I'm so, so sorry. I didn't realise. I couldn't have known . . .'

'Well, you should have known,' Ben said harshly. 'It

was obvious. If terrorists can use social media, so can poachers. I don't ever want to speak to you again. This friendship is over. You can wait for Saf. I'm going to the sanctuary. Glen can take me to the station. I'm catching the train back to Cape Town.'

He grabbed his rucksack and swung round.

'Ben, wait! Behind you!'

But it was too late. There was a loud hiss, like a deflating football, followed by a brown blur. Ben yelped with pain. The fat beige coils of a puff adder, its diamond markings unmistakable, slid beneath a rock.

Ben sat down dizzily and pulled up his cargo pants. There were two puncture marks above his ankle. Watery blood and venom oozed out. 'I've been bitten, Martine. I've been bitten.'

23

Martine had been in many challenging situations in her short life, but she couldn't ever remember feeling so helpless. More people died from puff adder bites than those of any other snake in Africa. Mambas and cobras were more deadly but puff adders were more abundant and slower to get out of the way. Their venom was among the most toxic of all vipers. Just 100 milligrams could kill a healthy adult within twenty-five hours. How much did Ben have in his system? Half of that? Double or triple that? There was no way of knowing.

Within a minute, Ben's left leg had swollen to the size

of Jabu's. It was aubergine with bruises. Blood blisters spread across his skin. Martine had taken off his boots and put his sweatshirt over him to keep him warm. She knew from the survival training she'd done with Tendai that puff adder venom was cytotoxic; it destroyed cells. Applying a tourniquet to Ben's leg could result in gangrene or even the loss of his foot. The best that she could do was lie him down and make sure that his heart was lower than the limb.

Ben was in agony and had already been violently sick. Between gasps, he begged Martine to forgive him for being so cruel to her.

'I don't know what . . . c-came . . . over me . . . It . . . wasn't . . . your . . . fault.'

'Ben, don't worry about it and don't waste energy talking. It's important that you keep still and calm. Try twiddling your toes to keep the blood flowing in your foot. Forget about everything else. None of it matters.'

Ben gave a violent shudder. Sweat ran like rain down his face. 'It . . . matters to . . . me. Martine, you're my . . . best . . . friend.'

'And you're mine,' she said, but she was talking to herself. Slumped against the boulder, Ben had lost consciousness.

A Cape Vulture swooped from the heavens and perched on a nearby tree like a winged judge, watching the drama unfold.

Martine was in a panic. She could stay with Ben and hope that a tourist with a phone came up the mountain to watch the sunset, or she could run down to the hotel and attempt to find a caretaker or builder who could help. But what if she made the wrong decision? What if Ben died while she was gone?

Grace's words came flooding back to her: *'One thing I can promise is that your gift will never leave you.'*

'But it did! It has!' Martine had insisted.

'No, chile, you left your gift. There's a thorn in your heart that's blocking your healing energy. It ain't real, it's just in your mind.'

'But what can I do to change that? Can you remove the thorn?'

'Ain't nothin' I nor anybody else can do. It will come out only when it's ready. When you believe . . . *'*

Martine kneeled beside Ben and put her hands over the blood-stained gauze she'd used to cover the wound. All she had to do was *believe.*

She thought about the night she'd gone out into the rainy darkness to find a white giraffe everyone had told her existed only in her imagination. The connection she'd found with Jemmy had lit a fire in her heart. Healing was an exchange of energies. Jemmy had saved her, then she'd saved him. She'd stood up for Ben in a fight against school bullies and it was his bravery and knowledge of ships that had allowed her to rescue Jemmy from the hunters who'd stolen him.

Love. It made life worth living.

A familiar heat began to course around her body. Previously, she'd only ever used her healing gift on animals. Now she needed to save her best friend's life.

Stronger and stronger the electrical charge pulsed through her.

Above her head, the Cape Vulture brooded.

When Ben's breathing steadied, Martine stood up. The wound had stopped leaking and the colour had returned to his skin, but she couldn't take a chance that she'd done enough. She had to find a way to call the emergency services. The only solution she could think of was to make a flag that might attract the attention of a park ranger.

It took her under five minutes to reach the top of Brandwag's Buttress. In the light of the setting sun, the sandstone cliffs glowed an electric orange. Down in the valley, dots moved. Hikers! Martine knotted her sweatshirt to a stick. Her hands were shaking. She was terrified that Ben might regain consciousness and think she'd abandoned him.

'Everything all right, Miss? Can I assist you?'

Like a mirage, a ranger was approaching, rifle in hand. 'Yes!' cried Martine. 'Yes, you can assist me! My friend has been bitten by a snake.'

The man recoiled. 'What snake? Where?'

'A puff adder. Come, I'll show you where I left Ben.'

The ranger stood unmoving. 'Is he . . . dead?'

'No, he's not,' snapped Martine. 'but he will be if we don't act fast. Please can I borrow your phone? It's an extreme emergency.'

'Where's your park permit?' demanded the man, suddenly aggressive.

'You're worried about a permit when my friend could die or lose his leg unless he gets to A&E? We can talk about money and park tickets as soon as I know that the emergency sevices are on their way.'

The ranger cocked his rifle. 'You're lying. I know what you're up to. You're one of the kids I've been hearing about. You're in league with some poachers. Which gang is it? Where is the rhino with the giant horn?'

A tsunami of ice rushed through Martine's veins. In her anxiety about Ben, she hadn't noticed that the ranger's shirt was a size too small for him and had circles of sweat beneath the armpits. Real rangers tended to use weapons that were cheap, battered and sometimes decades old. This man's gun looked as if it was fresh out of a munitions factory. She was able to observe its shiny barrel at close quarters because by then it was pointing directly at her.

'If you recognize the worm that is the lust for rhino gold in the eyes of any man, woman, boy or girl,' Grace had told her, *'don't be brave. Don't try to stand in their way. Just run.'*

Easier said than done.

'I don't know what you're talking about. I came here with my friend to watch the sunset. Now he's been bitten. All I care about is—'

'Enough about the snake!' The poacher's finger twitched on the trigger. 'I want to know where your gang has put the rhino with the long horn. I'm going to count to three. If you don't give me the right answer, I'm going to shoot.'

'I wouldn't do that if I were you,' said Ben, materialising like an apparition from a ghost story. His elephantine leg was the purple of nightmares and his clothes were covered in watery blood and dirt, but somehow he was standing. The poacher gawped.

'You really don't want to go around shooting children. There's a hefty prison sentence attached to that.'

'Shut up!' ordered the poacher, recovering. He swung the rifle in Ben's direction. 'Tell me where the rhino is or you and your little friend are going to go flying without a parachute. No prison sentence for me then. The police will think it was an accident.'

Ben stepped in front of Martine. 'You leave my friend out of this. She can't tell you what she doesn't know. Let her go.'

'Do you want me to shoot you now?' demanded the poacher. 'Where is the rhino? Simple question.'

Bit by bit he forced them backwards to the edge of the cliff. Martine could feel the void sucking at her. She willed the ground beneath them to hold firm. It looked suspiciously crumbly.

'Why do you care?' raged the poacher. 'It's a dumb animal. It's not sweet like a kitten or puppy. Tell me where it is and you get to live. You're children. You've got years of happy times in front of you. Is one rhino's life worth more than yours?'

'Now *you're* lying,' said Martine. 'Even if we could tell you where this rhino with the long horn is, which we can't, you'll probably shoot us anyway. You kill rhinos because you measure their lives in gold. When you spend the dirty money that you get for your crimes, does it ever occur to you that far away in China, Vietnam, the Yemen or wherever, somebody's sick mum or dad or brother or wife is going to die because of you? They'll die because men like you send them powdered horn and tell them that something that's no different to your disgusting fingernails is going to cure their cancer or their liver disease or their brain tumour.

'Each horn gets broken up and sent to dozens of different herbal medicine shops or fake healers who prescribe it to hundreds of people. So every time you hack the horn off the rhino, it's not just that animal you kill, it's everyone who believes it will save them. It's not the rhino that's dumb, it's you. You're a murderer. You're—'

An immense gust of wind almost blew Martine and Ben off their feet. Fortunately, they stumbled forward and didn't topple backwards off the cliff. There was a deafening roar and a helicopter came blasting up over the side of the mountain. Leaning out of the door were Saf and Marius Goss. Dr Goss had a tranquiliser gun in his hand.

He took aim and a dart speared the poacher in the thigh. The man dropped his weapon with a yell of rage. His eyes crossed. Hands flailing, he collapsed to the ground. By the time the helicopter landed, he was snoring.

Ben's knees buckled. He sat down hard. Martine rushed over and put her arm around his shoulders.

'Not ... good ... for ... my ... reputation, being ... saved by a girl,' he mumbled weakly. 'Two girls, really. You and Saf.'

'Don't be daft,' said Martine. 'Saving friends is a two-way street. You've just offered to take a bullet for me. Dr Goss's *James Bond* helicopter trick was impressive and hugely welcome, but you'll always be my hero.'

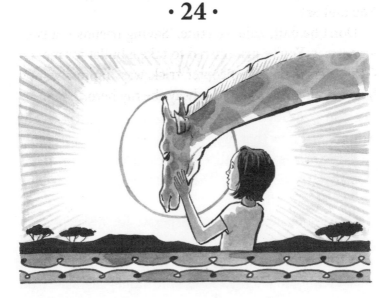

24

For Martine, almost the best part about getting home to Sawubona was discovering that Cleo had survived intensive care and was recuperating in the hospital behind the house. A famous wildlife vet had performed reconstructive surgery on her face. It would take her many months to make a full recovery, but in due course she'd get a prosthetic horn to replace the one the poachers took. It would be bright pink. In the meanwhile, Glen had sent Billy to keep her company.

'I'm convinced that the healing you did on Cleo after she was attacked is the reason she's alive today,' said Gwyn Thomas, giving Martine a hug. 'The vet told me he's never seen a rhino with injuries as critical as hers make such a rapid recovery. He said it was almost as if she'd been "kissed by an angel". His words, not mine.'

She knew little of her granddaughter's adventures in the Golden Gate Highlands. Glen and Susie had agreed with Martine and Ben that there was no sense in burdening anyone back in Cape Town with horror stories about their near-death encounters with armed gangs and cliff edges – not now that they were safe.

'Goodwin is gutted that Victor was involved with the poachers, but he's taking it better than expected,' Glen told them. 'He'd heard rumours that Victor had a gambling problem, but he'd been so desperate for his nephew to get a degree that he'd chosen to believe it wasn't true. Much harder for him to cope with was the revelation that Victor had planned to use the money he made from leading the poachers to Honey to pay off his debts. Victor knew that Goodwin had raised her from babyhood and loved her like a daughter. It was the ultimate betrayal. If his nephew had succeeded in killing her, I don't think Goodwin would have been answerable for consequences. As it is, he's encouraging his nephew to get help for his addiction. Whether or not Victor goes to jail, he'll be expelled from veterinary college.'

Victor's case was part of a fast-moving enquiry. The Python gang of poachers had been involved in both the Golden Gate Highlands and Sawubona attacks, but only by coincidence. They'd originally planned to kill Honey at her Mpumalanga reserve, but Dr Goss had whisked her away before they could get to her. They'd given up and were looking for a new target when Victor contacted them via the Dark Web, an alternative Internet site popular with criminals.

Detectives believed that the Dark Web was also the method Dirk Carswell had used to buy rhino horn. As far as they could tell, he'd negotiated a discount on the horn if he could pinpoint the location of some suitable rhinos for them. He did that by messaging the gang when Tendai stopped to show the visitors Cleo, Spartacus and their baby. The poachers then used the GPS on the manager's phone to get the exact coordinates for the attack just hours later.

As horrible as it was to know the details, Martine breathed a huge sigh of relief to have it officially confirmed that she was in no way responsible for what had happened. At the time the Tweet had gone out, their diabolical plan had already been in operation. There was nothing she or anyone else could have done to prevent it.

Sawubona's visitor rules had already been changed. From now on, all tourists would be required to switch off or surrender their phones before entering the reserve.

It was a cruel irony that, despite Dirk's efforts, Uncle Huynh had died of liver cancer less than five days after leaving Sawubona. Dirk faced a long prison sentence if convicted. He'd told reporters that he was resigning as Take Flight's manager to 'give me time to fight these outrageous allegations that are wholly without foundation'.

Up in her room, Martine used a roll of wide brown tape to seal the box on her bed. It was packed with books that she and Ben had collected for Saf. It weighed a ton and would cost a fortune to courier to the Golden Gate Sanctuary, but by the time Martine had finished explaining about Saf's dad and how fearless and brilliant she was, Gwyn Thomas was ready to dispatch her a whole library.

Which proved to Martine that for every wicked person in the world, there were thousands of noble ones. Take Dr Goss. He'd snatched them from the jaws of death and found a safe home for Honey and Jabu. It had been tough deciding whether to return the calf to his mum or keep him with Honey, with whom he'd bonded. In the end, Marius and Glen had taken the decision to send him to the secret sanctuary with his adopted mum. In the months and years to come, Dr Goss planned to relocate all of Glen's orphaned rhinos when they came of age. If their species was to be preserved, they'd be needed. Where he was taking them he wouldn't say.

'I could tell you but I'd have to kill you afterwards,' he'd joked. 'All I can say is that it's on an island with plenty of security and the last place on earth anyone would think to look for them. If humans ever come to their senses and no longer feel the need to slaughter these special creatures for their body parts, we might consider moving them back to Africa. Until then, we're going to concentrate our efforts on keeping the gene pool strong and our rhinos alive and happy.'

Transporting rhinos across the globe cost a king's ransom but FAW had been helped by an unlikely source. Lars, the Belgium hunter, had donated over a million dollars to the charity. The experience of watching

Jabulani play at Sawubona had, he told Dr Goss, caused him to give up hunting and devote his life to saving wild creatures. Never again did he want to rob a baby animal of its mother or be the thief of its joy.

Lying on her bed, Martine read an email from Saf, written on the new laptop given to her by Dr Goss. The head of FAW had been so impressed by Saf's coded message, which had allowed him to rescue two children, two rhinos and a goat, that he'd offered her a scholarship to one of South Africa's best schools. If she did well in her exams, a job at FAW would be waiting for her when she came out. If she 'borrowed' things and played truant, she'd be returning to live with her aunt.

I don't think he means it, wrote Saf, *but I wouldn't want to test him. Say hi to Ben for me and tell him I hope his leg gets better soon. Good luck with starting high school next week. Don't lose a minute's sleep. You and Ben survived gun-toting maniacs, snake bites, frenzied rhinos, a crazed veterinary student and ... me. Can anything be more scary than that?*

Love and hugs,
Your friend, Saf x

Martine typed back:
You're absolutely right. Nothing can top that! Thanks for everything. We owe you.

Go get 'em, girl. So proud of you. Smile, stay strong and believe.

Love and hugs,
Your friend, Martine x

'Martine, you've got to come and see this,' Gwyn Thomas called up the stairs.

Martine went down reluctantly. She knew what was on TV and she didn't want to see it. Given a choice, she'd have been racing across the game reserve on Jemmy.

'Take Flight are performing live in Paris,' said her grandmother, sounding ridiculously excited, considering she was in her seventies. 'They're really very talented, these boys. It's hard to believe that they visited Sawubona barely two weeks ago and we all dined by candlelight on the escarpment. So much has happened since then, to them and to us.

'According to the newspapers, Jayden is devastated by the revelations about Dirk. He fell in love with Africa and with the rhino at Sawubona in particular. This has hit him very hard. Tiffany, their PR person, was interviewed earlier and said that when the Paris concert is over Jayden's taking an extended break for medical reasons. Meaning stress, I suppose. Such a shame. It's not his fault that his manager became obsessed and deluded in his zeal to repay Uncle Huynh's favour. I hope Jayden bounces back soon. Such a charming young man and what a gorgeous voice he has.'

In spite of herself, Martine was drawn into the show. The part of her that Jayden's music and lyrics had touched after her mum and dad died was still there. He could still move her.

When it was over, she went outside to find Ben. He was grooming Shiloh beside the paddock fence.

'How's your leg?' asked Martine.

He glanced up with a smile. 'Almost perfect, thanks to you. The hospital I went to in Clarens, near Golden Gate, has phoned my mum and dad twice wanting to know if I'll go back to take part in a special study. They analysed a sample from the bite area on my ankle and the tissue was mostly healthy. They can't understand it. Even when my leg was massive and swollen, they said that it was as if some mysterious chemical was fighting the effects of the venom. The doctor was quite disturbed by it. I explained that I'd been healed by my best friend, but when he questioned me and I said you were the same age as me and not an experienced *sangoma,* he dismissed me as the type of boy who believes in elves.'

Ben put down the dandy brush, his dark eyes suddenly serious. 'I could feel it, Martine, the energy from your hands. It went through me like a fire tornado. At the same time it was incredibly gentle and ... loving. The pain just dissolved. Afterwards, I could hear you getting up and moving away. I wanted to call out and thank you, but I couldn't move or open my eyes.'

'You got up when it mattered and distracted the poacher,' said Martine. 'You probably saved both our lives. I'm glad I helped you too. I wasn't sure if my gift would work on a human or whether it would work at all. When I thought I might lose you, it was the worst feeling in the world.'

He grinned. 'Martine Allen, don't you know by now

183

that you're stuck with me? One thing you're never going to do is lose me.'

'Promise?'

'Promise. Well, unless we're racing Shiloh and Jemmy. Then all bets are off.'

Martine followed his gaze. Jemmy was strolling up from the waterhole, his white and silver coat glowing against the sunset. They walked to the fence to greet him, followed by the Basotho pony.

'Are you saying you want a rematch even though we pipped you to the post the last time?' Martine teased.

'I'm saying that the forecast for tomorrow is twenty-five degrees and blue skies. It might be fun to have breakfast up on the escarpment. If there's no one around when we come down and if Jemmy and Shiloh want to stretch their legs as they cross the plain, who are we to stop them?'

Martine couldn't help laughing. 'You're on.'

The four friends stood together as the sun bowed out in a blaze of glory. Martine, who had one arm around Shiloh and the other resting on Jemmy's soft muzzle, had Jayden's new song stuck on repeat in her head. Every time she recalled his final words at the Paris concert, her heart swelled with a complex mix of emotions. But most of all she felt hope.

'This goes out to every wild animal that is tonight in pain, in a cage or the target of poachers, circus owners or any other kind of exploitation,' Jayden had said, leaning into the microphone. 'We hear them, we feel for them and we want you to join with us in fighting for a better future for them. This is our freedom song.'

Morning on the Serengeti, a lion greets the rising sun
The leopard and the Springbok dream, a cheetah's on the
*   run*
Across the world their brother's life
A hell on earth of pain and strife
The cage slams shut, that's when the nightmare begins

What have we done
What're we gonna do about it
When the last rhino's dead and gone
Will we ask where we went wrong?
The only hope is if we learn to say
Freedom is the only way
It's not too late to right what's wrong
If we sing a freedom song

The lights go up in Vegas, a tiger jumps through the fire
A dancing bear has tears in her eyes, a monkey collared
*   in wire*
Across the world a better life
Waits for those allowed to fly
The cage door opens, that's when the magic begins

What have we done
What're we gonna do about it

When the last rhino's dead and gone
Will we ask where we went wrong?
The only hope is if we learn to say
Freedom is the only way
It's not too late to right what's wrong
If we sing a freedom song

If we don't wake up and learn to love
We'll lose this precious gift of the wild
No, it doesn't take a lot to see
There's only one way to be and that's free
Born free, forever free